Chris
I've loved getting to know you. Can't wait for the next book

Scarlett

Also by Suzette Vaughn
From Beckoning Books

Mortals, Gods and a Muse

Badeaux Knights

By

Suzette Vaughn

Beckoning Books

Published by Second Wind Publishing

Kernersville

Beckoning Books
Second Wind Publishing, LLC
931-B South Main Street, Box 145
Kernersville, NC 27284

This book is a work of fiction. Names, characters, locations and events are either a product of the author's imagination, fictitious or use fictitiously. Any resemblance to any event, locale or person, living or dead, is purely coincidental.

Copyright © 2008 by Suzette Vaughn

All rights reserved, including the right of reproduction in whole or part in any format.

First Beckoning Books edition published August, 2008. Beckoning Books, Running Angel, and all production design are trademarks of Second Wind Publishing, used under license.

For information regarding bulk purchases of this book, digital purchase and special discounts, please contact the publisher at www.secondwindpublishing.com

Front cover design by Suzette Vaughn

Manufactured in the United States of America

ISBN 978-1-935171-06-5

Every woman needs her knight in shining armor. This is to the ones in my life through the years.

—Suzette Vaughn

1.

The early Mississippi morning matched Sonja's mood: dark, gray, and temperamental—especially for February.

She took a much-needed deep breath as her late-model soft white Jetta rolled to a stop next to the other two vehicles in the gravel driveway. Putting it in park, her eyes skimmed the two-story house. It felt like home, as always, even if she had never lived there.

The ancient farmhouse, hand-built sometime in the late 1800's, with its broad front porch added in the early part of the 20th century in true Victorian style, still boasted the original decorative molding. For five generations the Badeaux family lived here, worked here, played here, loved here, and died here. Every Badeaux treated the old homestead like a member of the family, taking care of it and treasuring it until the day it passed on to their children or grandchildren.

Too bad the only legacy my family left was heartache.

For over a century, the soft chocolate brown exterior and royal blue hurricane shutters had remained the same. Two rockers sat empty on the front porch, a new coat of stain every now and again keeping them youthful beyond their years. The barn, quietly aging as it sat off in the back, only needed a can of traditional red paint to give it new life.

A new life is exactly what I need.

The perfectly manicured front yard displayed shrubs and bushes all in matching shapes and sizes. When spring arrived, they would be full of azalea blossoms of fuchsia, soft pink, purple, and white. The old trees grew wherever they wanted, their arms reaching to the sky and trimmed only enough to keep their leafy fingers inches from touching the roof. The warmth and security of the house called to her.

Reliability and love unlike anything else in my life.

Sonja wished she could have grown up here, in this family, or somewhere just like it. At twenty-three, she remained single with no children. Instead of a family, she had chosen a good job and a good education. Her three sisters thought she had gone off the deep end when she left Memphis to go to school in Mississippi. They assumed she would get married and have babies like they did, especially when her mother died two weeks after her high school graduation. Instead, she worked her way through college, concentrating on her studies to distract her from her hardships.

A harsh sigh escaped as she pulled her eyes from the house to look in the rearview mirror.

Now I can add "easily distracted" to my list of faults, right along with "temperamental". As long as "erratic" and "overly emotional" doesn't hit that list, I might survive this.

Though nothing else filled her mind since midnight—at least not to any extent—she still couldn't figure out what to say. The clock moved to six. Although she didn't remember the time passing, she doubted it was wrong. She didn't have to worry about arriving too early. Just too late. *Way too late.*

As she straightened her sunglasses, it crossed

her mind to apply makeup. Discarding the thought as quickly as it appeared, she ran her hand through her windblown hair, grabbed her bag, and stepped out into the cool morning air.

A smile briefly crossed her face as she made her way through the wet grass and ankle deep fog. Her life was about to change for good or bad. Opening the screen door, she knocked. It really wasn't necessary. Not needing to wait for an answer she pushed open the unlocked front door, stepping in and patting the reliable wood when the hinges didn't squeak. As Sonja let her bag drop to the hardwood floor, she scanned the room spread out before her.

The L-shaped mahogany staircase crested the length of the room, the steps worn by time, yet as sturdy as the day they were built. To the right, at the foot of the staircase, was the dining area. The centerpiece of the room was a beautiful mahogany drop-leaf table surrounded by four chairs. With leaves added in and the ends folded out, the table became a large oval, comfortably seating twelve—or more for a close family like the Badeaux's. She could picture the big family dinners eaten at that table. How easy it was to imagine the expansive table covered in favorite family foods, woven placemats, cloth napkins, real silverware, and delicate bone china.

Along the far right wall stood the grandfather clock that kept time as precisely as any digital timepiece. Closer to her was the sitting area, which hadn't changed in probably fifty years or more. The room was intentionally decorated to make guests feel welcome. The entire house gave her that feeling. To her left was the living room. The new leather couch seemed out of place in the midst of the antique furniture that adorned the house so magnificently.

She glimpsed movement at the corner of her eye and turned her head to look at the archway on the other side of the dining area. It was Kaleb—"Kale." She caught her breath. He was a marvelous sight, six feet tall, trim and muscular in a long sleeved T-shirt and Dockers. His broad shoulders filled the archway. His hair, still the same shiny brown mess, was longer than she remembered. His eyes, his best feature because they spoke to her and emotions poured forth from them, if anyone was perceptive enough to notice. At the moment, they expressed adoration and confusion.

She couldn't meet his smile with one of her own.

Before Kale had a chance to say anything, a noise from the top of the staircase pulled Sonja's attention from his questioning hazel eyes. Nicolas bounded down the stairs to his brother's left. Almost a mirror image of his younger sibling, Nick was an inch taller and more muscular—a fact made apparent by the still unbuttoned black dress shirt that was obvious to her even halfway across the house. The same rich brown hair glinted with a mutiny of colors in a cleaner, more styled cut than his brother's. The eyes that met hers were also the same as the pair into which she had been staring, except they were more intense and less whimsical, as the emotions within them were being restrained.

"What're you doin' here this early? Actually, what're you doin' here at all?" Nick grinned as he leaned against the banister.

She was more breathtaking to Nick each time he saw her—not that he ever told anyone she affected him that way. Her rich brown leather jacket partially covering the deep neckline of her red sweater that topped the nicest pair of blue jeans he'd seen since the last time his eyes fell on her. Her shoulder length, wavy black hair was messier than usual and hung over part of her face. Sunglasses hid eyes deeper and darker than a cup of his brother's strongest coffee. Her rigid stance was unusual. Normally she was a relaxed person. Something was wrong with his Sonja.

Not knowing what else to do or say, not wanting them to start throwing questions she wasn't ready to answer, Sonja simply pushed her sunglasses up on her head, pulling her hair away from her face. She couldn't meet the eyes of the brothers frozen in silence.

When they saw what she hid behind her hair and glasses, their smiles quickly faded. The entire left side of her face was swollen black and blue.

Kale was the first one to speak. "He's a dead man."

Nick's eyes changed. The blood he wanted to spill burning within them. His jaw tightened, too angry to speak. Each step across the open room echoed like the executioner stalking to the gallows.

Kale's forearms strained, his veins bulging with the abundant adrenaline coursing through them.

"Nicolas! Kaleb!" Her voice came out stronger than she expected, her heart pounding with each footstep. "Don't!"

"Not this time, Sonja." Nick found his voice, drowning out every other noise in the house.

"Don't even try." Kale added.

"He's already in the hospital," she said, hoping reason would prevail

"We can make it worse." Nick shot back, grabbing his coat with one hand, the other already on the door.

Sonja put a hand on Nick's chest, trying to wedge her body between him and the door, knowing she didn't have the strength to stop him on her best day.

"What are you gonna do? Break bones that are already broken?" If she could control Nick, Kale would be easy.

"For a start, yeah!" Nick couldn't open the door unless he hit her with it, which was absolutely out of the question.

"He has twenty-something stitches in his head and three broken ribs."

"I knew you would make him pay someday." Kale said, his lips quirked into a smile.

"We're gonna make sure he can't do it again." Nick said, still gripping the doorknob tensely.

Kale put his hands on her waist. Sonja wrapped both hands around Nick's arm as Kale lifted her off the floor. Her voice grew stronger with each word, more of her untapped temperamental power surfacing.

"I came here to see about your extra room, not for you to go off half-cocked for vengeance."

When she was sure Kale had a good hold on her waist, she wrapped her legs around him, keeping her hands locked around Nick's arm. Neither would get away easily unless they wanted to pull her in half.

Staring at Sonja's hands that securely held his arm, Nick's anger urged him to pull away while his heart said 'don't move'. "I don't do anything half-cocked, darlin'."

"You'll end up in jail." Sonja held both of them as tight as her tired muscles allowed.

"That's what lawyers are for," Nick said through clenched teeth, as his brother gave a good tug.

Sonja squeezed tighter. "What happens if you're in jail when he gets out of the hospital and comes after me?"

"He can't come after you if he's dead." Nick

stated without a moment of hesitation.

Sonja spoke softly, her voice pleading. She couldn't yell. She couldn't demand anymore. Her face hurt. Her heart hurt. She was tired of fighting.

"Then you'd be there even longer and your life would be ruined."

Nick's eyes shifted from her hand up the leather coat to her face. She was frightened. Not of him. *For* him. She didn't flinch, didn't look away as the intensity of his eyes burned into hers. Normally she would have done one of two things. Either given in, hoping one of them would come to their senses before they got to the hospital, or she would have cried. He could see the tears, but for now, they refused to fall. The pulse pounding through her fingers kept time with his. Sometime over the past few months she had discovered anger. Still the shy woman he always knew, but now with a fire that refused to be contained.

"I won't kill him," Nick said, "if you promise me you won't go back to him."

"Deal." It was a bargain she quickly made, having already decided on her own that she wouldn't go back. If it made Nick feel better and calmed him down, to think he had swayed her decision, then she wouldn't argue.

No one moved. She considered her position, concerned his body was still too tight. "Nick, let go of the door."

Nick let his hand slip off the doorknob, catching her upper half in a tight hug. He sandwiched her in between himself and Kale. Understanding she needed the love. Happy she lived in spite of Jerry's savagery. She'd survived his cheating on her. She'd survived him hitting her, twice that Nick knew of. She'd survived, at least so far.

Although being in a compressed position, Sonja tilted her face to look at Kale. "Do you agree not to kill him too?" she asked.

"As long as you keep holding me like this," Kale said, a wicked grin spreading over his face, "I'll agree to anything."

Nick relaxed as much as he could. He stepped back and released her, expecting his brother to do the same. Nick smacked his brother's shoulder when Kale didn't follow suit. "Put her down."

"But I'm enjoyin' this." Kale smiled, his eyes full of ornery thoughts.

She almost smiled as a giggle escaped. "Put me down, ya big lug."

Kale gently put her feet back on the ground. Nick walked around them to sit on the couch, unable to hide the aggression in his voice as he spoke.

"If you won't let us kill him, you can at least explain what happened."

Sonja moved to the couch with Kale following. She sat in the middle with a brother on each side. Kale studied the ugly black and blue marks marring her face.

"He got in a good right hook." She shrugged to imply the entire ordeal was no big deal. "I grabbed the closest thing to me, which happened to be a porcelain lamp and I hit him over the head. He fell to the floor and I kicked until he stopped movin'. Broke his head. Broke the lamp, too." She sighed. "I liked that lamp."

"Why did he hit you?" Nick didn't mean to badger her. He had so much pent up anger he could only control it by chastising himself.

Stubbornly, she lifted her chin. A flash of anger crossed her face, the new fire in her Nick had just discovered. "It was just a fight. I got in his way."

She was keeping too much from them. Still,

Nick was afraid to open his mouth after her reaction to his last question. Kale interrupted the silence quickly enough.

"Well, I'm really proud that you fought back this time."

"Thanks." She rolled her eyes. "When do ya'll need to leave for work?"

Kale glanced across the room to the elderly grandfather clock. "I should've left ten minutes ago, when you walked through the door."

"Go before the boss gets mad." She almost smiled again.

"You know I'd *hate* to get fired." He couldn't say it with a straight face. Kale had opened his own landscaping company two and a half years before. He loved working with his hands and getting dirty. Sonja thought it added to his easy-going charm.

Kale stood, about to be late for the first time ever. The guys working for him were surely going to dish out grief.

"You, young lady, lock up when Nick leaves and don't touch any lamps." He kissed her forehead then grabbed his jacket on his way out the door.

Sonja watched until the door closed, then turned to find Nick staring at her. Relieved to see the fury in his eyes was mostly dissipated, she naturally reverted into her former shy self. She was happy to know that part of her still existed. "Young lady?" she huffed, "He's only three months older than me."

Nick put his hand on her chin, slowly moving her face to where he could look at the bruising. She tried to stop him, but she realized it was useless. Sooner or later, he would get a good look at the damage. His voice wasn't as harsh but it wasn't the friendly tone that she needed, "Did you put an ice pack on that?"

"I kept a bag of carrots pushed against my face until the police left."

"Police were there too? You didn't share that part of your little story. What else did you leave out?" They stubbornly eyed each other.

"Nothing of importance. Aren't there computers somewhere waiting for you?" Nick chose a career as a computer technician to keep his mind busy. His brain worked a lot like hers...technical, methodical, and fast.

"Yeah there are. I guess I should get goin'. Of course, I could call in sick." His voice had finally lightened.

"Not on my account you won't." Her strong voice appeared again. By the look on his face, he liked the new Sonja. That was a relief she would thank him for someday.

"You don't need to be alone today."

With a light sigh, she found her softness again. "I have boxes in the car, and more I can go back and get. At some point, I'm sure I'll need sleep."

"I don't like it."

"Your opinion is duly noted." Although softer, her voice was still too heated.

"Watch the attitude, *young lady*. This is still my house."

"Won't forget that for as long as I live." The smile on his face said it all. She was there and he couldn't be happier. She couldn't help but watch as he stood, then offered his hand to her. He pulled her up, kissing her bruised cheek as gently as possible.

"Do like Kale said and lock up."

"Yes, Daddy." She mimicked a spoiled daughter.

He shot back a stern look as he grabbed his jacket. "If you're not careful, you'll get grounded."

"Go to work," came out a little exasperated.

"You can't kick me out of my own house." Nick was still considering taking a sick day.

"Wouldn't dream of it." She headed out the door in front of him.

"Where do you think you're goin'?" The firm, fatherly tone was back as he followed her.

"Getting boxes out of my car before I fall asleep. Aren't you going to work?"

"I could stay and help."

She planted her hand on her hip and sternly tilted her head. Considering her stance for a moment, Nick gave up. "Guess I'm going to work."

He slowly pulled out of the drive, stopping for a second as he watched her pull a box out of her car. Sonja was home.

For three years, Kale and Nick tried to convince her that Jerry was a waste of her time. She deserved better. Nick smiled slightly as he drove. Now they had her away from him. The only question was how long could they keep her away? He and Kale each loved her in his own way. It had been so since they first met her. Together, they treated her as a sister only because they didn't know how else to act with her.

The now-hospitalized Jerry cheated on her constantly. One night at a club, he and Kale discovered Jerry being overly friendly with a blonde. They cornered Jerry that night and threatened him with dismemberment, but it didn't do much good. Rumors ran rampant that Jerry continued his cheating habits with one floozy after another while Sonja continued to blindly trust him. Without rock-solid proof, they couldn't tell her. She would be hurt and she wouldn't leave him based only on their suspicions.

A year earlier Jerry hit Sonja in a drunken rage and she appeared at their door. That time, she stayed with the brothers for a week, spending her time talking both of them out of going and giving him a taste of his own medicine. Even with the numerous threats on her life, including one indicating the house would mysteriously burn down, Jerry somehow convinced her to return to him. This time, if she returned, he would have to let her go, not matter what it did to his heart. This time he wouldn't be able to let her come home.

As she finished unloading the car, exhaustion crept through Sonja's veins. Though she yearned to lie down and sleep, necessity drove her to get in the car and go back to the apartment. She slid the key into the lock with a deep breath. The sun shone through the sliding glass door that opened out onto the patio. Everything in the place reminded her of the time she spent with Jerry. The pictures of them together on the mantel. His and Hers bath towels hanging on the rod. The broken, bloody lamp still on the floor. Stepping around it, she hustled to finish packing.

She met Jerry while still in college. Somehow, he made her feel special, unlike anyone before. He was handsome, smooth and wanted to take care of her. Within six months of meeting, he told her they would get married. She could quit college and take care of their children. College was important to her, so she forced herself to tell him no and to keep saying it every time since.

Before leaving the apartment, she double-checked that everything was in boxes by the door. When she brought the brothers with her later, it would be a quick grab and go. With the lights out, she slammed the door behind her, smiling—as much as her bruises would let her—all the way home.

Relieved to be back at the Badeaux home, she unpacked what she could from the car before the lack of sleep took its final toll. The feeling of safety caused the slight sleep depravation to be even worse.

Understanding how Goldilocks felt, she tried to find somewhere to sleep. First, she chose the new couch in the living room. It was close enough to the door that she could hear when someone came home. She grabbed her jacket to cover up with, too tired to find a blanket and waste time searching though every closet. It didn't take long to decide that it was not the best choice. She kept sticking to the leather. Abandoning the modern couch, she moved over to the antiquity in the corner. This second choice looked to be older than the house.

In less than two minutes, she got up from the cloth-covered pile of rocks she mistook for a sofa. Yawning, she shuffled towards the kitchen. The old-world charm of the room wasn't lost when the brothers replaced the old appliances with new stainless steel. They also added the butcher's block in the center of the room for a versatile island. The laundry room had a door from the kitchen, as did a half bath that was stuffed behind the staircase.

Passing the island, she made her way to the sink and filled a glass with fresh water. Enjoying the cool liquid, she marveled at the fields outside the picture window. The simplicity of the view and the purity of well water were never lost on her. A simple life. Another yawn escaped as she set the glass on the counter before padding her way back through the dining room. She held the banister as she went, her feet dragging up the solid mahogany steps leading to the four rooms on the second floor.

The first door up the stairs opened to Kale's room. Pushing open the door, she braced for the worst.

The room resembled a pigsty, as always. The four sets of floor-length windows made the room appear larger even with the already immense space. The deep rust-colored blanket hung mostly off the king size bed that looked dwarfed in the space against the interior wall. The bathroom on the other side of the bed was something else the boys added when they came home. She carefully closed the door and moved on, afraid of what might be lurking in the mess. Like the stray python he lost shortly after moving in.

Glancing down the length of the T-shaped hallway she could see straight to her bathroom, the only full bath until the brothers renovated the house. The tile was still original, white with a blue tile offset every few feet. It was a relief not to have to share the bathroom with the brothers—unless they wanted a bath. And if she wanted a shower she would simply have to use one of theirs. On the left of the bathroom was her unfurnished room slowly filling with boxes. On the right, the library that now more resembled a computer office than a room of solace where someone would sit quietly.

On the way to the end of the main hall, she looked over pictures of the brothers' family. Photographs lined every inch from where the stairs started to both ends of the hallway. She picked the boys out of pictures at all different ages. The only pictures she could remember of her own childhood had been taken at school.

Nick's room was the opposite of Kale's in layout and in cleanliness. It was neat as always. Nick was probably the only guy she knew that kept his room immaculate. She was pretty sure he even dusted. His bed sat against the outside wall somewhat covering two of the large windows instead of blocking the path to his bathroom. The bathrooms were identical, small, just enough for a shower, toilet, and basin.

Remembering how nice Nick's bed felt the last time she came to this house for refuge she pulled back the deep gray blanket and sheet. Tomorrow she would go buy a new bed, but for now his was the most familiar. She looked at Nick's collection of swords knowing she could grab one if anything happened.

Feeling secure for the first time in a year she snuggled down in his covers, drifting off to sleep within a few minutes.

Nick arrived home to find her car in the driveway, happy it was real—not a dream or hallucination. On the other hand, the bruise on her face was something he wished was just imaginary. Quickly ascending the porch, he almost hit his head on the door when it didn't open, until he remembered that they both told her to lock it. Fishing through his keys, he went through six before finding the right one. His watch confirmed the grandfather clock was still running on time, ten after four. He slowed his pace as he reached the stairs, not wanting to wake her up. Kale's room was too messy for human inhabitants, so he continued down the hall to his own room.

There she lay curled up in his bed. Her hair flowing over his pillow. Her fingers twined around the edge of his blanket. His brain creating possibilities of what he could do to Jerry for every iota of pain he ever caused her. Time slipped away as he watched her sleep, until he realized in amazement he lost seventeen minutes just staring at her. He shook his head, silently moving through the hall to her new room.

It had always been her room, just waiting on her to claim it. Boxes lining one wall delighted him. The last time she showed up, she only had one bag. He found her keys sitting on a stack of boxes and dropped them in his pocket. He kept busy with chores until it was almost time for his brother to arrive. Then he went outside to the driveway and waited.

Jumping off the trunk of his Mustang, Nick was talking before his brother could get out of his Durango. "Lets go make sure she got everything from that apartment."

"Where is she?" Kale said. "I want to take a shower before we take off."

"Asleep in my bed. We're gonna leave her there. God knows she needs the rest."

"When we are done getting her things from the apartment are we going to visit the hospital?" Kale questioned as his brother climbed in the passenger side. Giving up on getting a shower, he put the Dodge in reverse.

After a few seconds of silence, Nick shifted in his seat trying to keep his face from his brother.

"Not sure." Nick didn't have much to say, but his mind was going nonstop. Going to jail for killing Jerry wouldn't do anyone any good. Least of all Sonja. Spending his life in jail wouldn't be good either, no matter how satisfying putting the bastard in the ground would be.

"I think we should get it over with." Kale knew the anger would eat at Nick until he exploded if they didn't.

It didn't take long for the brothers to clean out the apartment of anything and everything that was hers, or they thought could be hers. Most of it was already in boxes. They loaded up Kale's SUV then headed to the hospital.

Kale smiled nicely at the receptionist in the

lobby, flirting a little while Nick stood by the elevators trying to act inconspicuous and control his temper. Kale thanked the receptionist for the room number and joined his brother as the elevator arrived. Up three floors Kale kept at least a little bit of the smile on his face as they passed nurses and doctors. The last thing they needed was someone stopping Nick, not just yet.

2.

Rita Wilkins sat at the nurses' desk. Just starting her shift, she grabbed the file with the list of her patients and hoped her teenage son was really at the movies like he said. She didn't want a repeat of last night when he went to a party instead of being home where he was supposed to be. Rita left work at ten to pick him up when the party turned violent. She lost too much income for missing half her shift. Being a single mom from the time her son was born meant every penny always counted.

In love and happy at eighteen, her world turned upside down when her boyfriend found out she was pregnant. Suddenly he didn't want her or their child. He chose to express this through his fists. She left with a bloody nose and a black eye and never looked back. Now she was still beautiful, but no longer a delicate flower. More than once her son called her into the backyard—and lost.

Rita momentarily forgot about her son as Dana sat on the desk beaming at her. Rita couldn't resist asking, "Child, what you smilin' about?"

Dana reminded Rita of herself before the birth of her baby. The pair worked together for almost four years and Rita couldn't help but mother the girl.

"You are gonna just love our new patient."

"Is Mr. Lane a bad patient?" Rita raised one eyebrow in suspicion.

"We kept him drugged enough that he isn't too bad, but up until about three hours ago the cops were sitting outside his room."

This didn't shock Rita. Not much did. Most of their patients were drive-by victims, drunk car crashes, or random gun wounds. Victims of the worst that people could do to each other, which made officers of the law a normal sight in their waiting room. The nurses gave the same care no matter how their patients got there, but the stories they shared helped them deal with the blood and violence and even death. "Why this time?"

"He hit his girl and she didn't take it well." Dana waited. Rita's eyes rose, giving Dana her full attention. "Officer Marshall said they got in a fight. He hit her. She took a lamp to his head and kicked him until he quit movin'."

"My kinda girl."

"Thought you would like that. She kicked him so hard we had to put him in traction. Afraid his back was messed up. Of course, the doctor got the results about two hours ago. The jerk's back is fine, but I haven't removed the traction yet."

"Letting him fret a bit are you?"

"Well, last time I went in he asked what the hell I was looking at, like I didn't need to be in there."

"Why did Officer Marshall leave?"

"Said the judge set his bail and his mommy paid it."

Rita huffed, "I would have let him rot. You done with your rounds?"

"All except Mr. Lane. He's asleep still." Dana's eyes shifted, following someone coming down the hall. Rita assumed it was a good looking doctor until Dana looked back at her, motioning her head toward the hall.

Rita knew the look. Picking up the phone, she pushed the quick line for security then watched two young men walk by. One was dirty in work clothes and smiled at the nurses as they passed. The other didn't smile, didn't look away from the hall in front of him. Rita whispered into the phone, "Send Harry up."

"They're going into Mr. Lane's room. Are we gonna to let Harry take 'em out?"

"Not sure yet." Rita peeked around the corner, watching the smiling boy enter the room. "I don't know if they intend to do him harm, but might as well get Harry up here just in case."

Nick walked cautiously into the room, making sure there was no one else in there, except the man in the bed. He wasn't surprised and was more than happy to find the room void of people. He didn't know yet how this conversation would turn out and the fewer people that witnessed it the better. In the truck on the way over he gave Kale his debit card and pin number just in case he needed bail. Kale of course laughed. But he was perfectly serious.

Jerry was a wiry guy about two inches shorter than Nick. The bandages on his head hid his short dishwater hair. Despite his clean-cut appearance, something about Jerry never did sit quite right with Nick. The feeling started the first time he saw him, long before anything bad ever happened.

The large flower arrangement on the dresser across from the bed caught his eye. Beautiful orchids that Sonja had more often than not setting around her house or office. The tag read 'Love you, Nell.' Nell must have thought Jerry liked the flowers, not knowing it was Sonja's favorite.

Kale casually walked in since his brother hadn't

come out. When his eyes fell on Jerry he couldn't help but smile bigger. As his brother nodded to get this over with, Nick turned from the flowers.

The unsaid communications stopped as a short, burly, black nurse walked in. Nick leaned against the dresser as relaxed as he could while avoiding eye contact. Knowing his eyes would give away more than his body language.

Kale stood up straight. "Evening ma'am." he still couldn't get the smile off his face. Worrying it would give away the fact there would be no mourning over the man in the bed. The nametag identified her as Rita Wilkins, RN.

"Hello. You guys friends?" Rita asked, eyeing the pair suspiciously.

"You could say that if you wanted." Kale chose to speak quickly knowing Nick wouldn't be able to keep pleasant if those flowers had a woman's name on the tag. By the look on Nick's face, Kale was pretty sure it didn't have "mom" scrawled across the tag.

Nurse Wilkins looked each of them up and down as she checked the IV drip and bandages. "Am I going to need to call security?"

"We don't plan on causin' any trouble ma'am. Just need to talk to your patient." Kale figured the heavyset nurse could take care of any problems herself without any help from security. In this part of the hospital, she would have to move patients from bed to bed, which made her strong. Didn't help that she looked mean—until she smiled at Kale.

"She messed him up good." Rita's smile grew wider.

Kale let go of his grin barely keeping back the laugh. "She defended herself well."

"Mr. Lane?" Rita nudged him a little harder than

necessary. "Wake up."

She wanted to give the visitors as much time as they needed. The head of security, Harry, would be up in a minute if anything got out of hand.

Jerry's eyes opened, slowly focusing on the nurse above him.

"You have visitors Mr. Lane." Rita smiled as nicely as she could.

She slowly raised his bed. First Jerry saw Nick and then glanced over at Kale, whose smile didn't seem to set him at ease.

As Rita turned to leave the room, Jerry realized the situation he faced.

"Nurse!" The best he could do was to mumble the word out past his bandages.

Ignoring him, Rita walked to Nick. Although doing so made her nervous, she felt along the leather trench coat, making sure there was no gun hidden under it.

Nick stood still to give her every possibility to find if he had one.

Before leaving the room, she whispered to Kale. "Nothing too much or the security guard will have to haul him off."

"Thank you, ma'am." He leaned against the wall knowing his brother needed to vent all the anger.

"Who is Nell?" Nick started with no fluctuation in his voice knowing he could lose what little control he held on his temper.

"Fuck you!" Spittle flew from the corners of Jerry's mouth.

"You are in no position to speak that way Jerry." Nick inched closer and closer to the bed. His control slipping away as he moved forward. "I would say she's your current girlfriend. Your only girlfriend.

Because if you ever, *ever* come near Sonja again you will be very lucky to wake up in a hospital."

Jerry pushed the nurse button repeatedly until Nick pulled it from his clenched hand. "Do I make myself perfectly clear, *Mr. Lane*?"

"Go to hell. You see what she did to me? I might have spine damage."

"Did you see her face? She is done with you and this is the only time we will ever have a *discussion*. Next time you come near her, you won't have time to say anything."

Nick put the nurse button on the table well out of reach. He turned to walk away, until Jerry spoke, the tone of his words stopped Nick more than the words themselves.

"You know I'll get her back."

"Over my dead body." Nick added as he walked by the end of the bed and elbowed Jerry's traction cable out of place. "Oops."

Jerry let out as much of a scream as he could with the bandages wrapped around his head.

Kale wanted to explode from laughter as he watched his brother remove the card from the flowers and pick up the vase.

"Don't keep in touch." Kale added, following his brother out the door.

"Thank you again, ma'am." Kale smiled at the nurses and security guard directly in front of the door. None of whom could answer from laughing aloud as Nick walked down the hall with the flowers.

The ride home started quietly. Nick wanted to put his fist through something. Kale objected saying he liked his windshield. Kale couldn't help laughing every now and again with the realization that Sonja was home. Sonja put Jerry in the hospital and Nick didn't kill him. Finally, the laughter became contagious and Kale breathed easier as his brother joined him.

Arriving at the house, Nick grabbed the flower arrangement while Kale pulled the first box out of the truck.

Nick took the porch stairs two at a time, happy she would be inside. After all her keys were in his pocket. The flowers looked good on the dining room table as he headed up the stairs to his room. His bed was empty. His heart sank. Trying not to overreact, he went to her new room and found her putting her clothes in the closet

"Ah! The culprits who stole my keys return to the scene of the crime. Lucky I didn't call the detective I met last night and have ya'll handcuffed and thrown in jail." Her smile lit up the room as Nick tossed her the keys.

"You were sleepin', we decided you needed it. How is the unpacking goin'?"

Kale bumped Nick in the back with the box as he said, "Better if you'd move out of the doorway."

Nick turned and took the box from his brother, flashing an unsaid warning. Though the message was clear to let them talk, Kale decided to go after another box instead of putting his foot in his mouth, as usual.

Sitting the box down with the others, Nick continued. "Looks like we need to get you a bed. You can have mine for the night if you want it."

He noticed how well the make-up perfectly covered the bruises as she faced him. How many times she had done that and not told them, he wondered. How much it must hurt to cover.

"I can't kick you out of your bed again." She said it like there wasn't a bruise on her face. Like it was a normal conversation, everyday in this room.

Everything in him wanted to say they could share his room. He knew better. For three years he's held it in. He would keep doing just that until the time was right. Since he fell in love with Sonja, his dating life almost ceased to exist. No one ever measured up to her. Each relationship short-lived and frustrating. Especially since Jerry didn't deserve her.

"It's fine, I don't work tomorrow. What can I help with?"

"Why don't you help me with the few things left in the truck?" Kale put his foot on his brother's butt to push him out of the way this time.

Nick took the box from Kale, setting it carefully with the others before running down the stairs. Catching up to his brother, he landed a hard smack on Kale's head. The healthy scrimmage in the front yard ending quickly when Nick pinned Kale to the ground.

Dropping the box to the floor, Nick looked around. "That's all of it."

"Good! Tell your brother to get a shower." Sonja spoke before she saw Kale coming in the doorway.

"Are you saying I smell?"

"I'm saying you're dirty. Get a shower so I can take you two to eat."

"I can cook." Nick objected.

Kale slipped out of the room happy he could finally get the shower. He also didn't want to sit through a normal bickering match between the two.

"I can take you out to eat. No reason cooking this late and you deserve the treat for getting my stuff." Looking for her bathroom items, Sonja opened a box, pulling out the bathrobe with *Hers* written on the side.

31

"And a few things I didn't want to keep."

"Sorry, we assumed it was yours."

"It's mine but I don't want it." Nick took the fluffy robe from her hands, thinking of ways he could burn it as an effigy of her past life. The mental picture of Jerry going up in flames with it was satisfying.

Sonja opened another box. "Looks like it's not the only thing ya'll grabbed. Wanna hand me an empty box and we can trash it all?"

"Of course," he said a little to happy to comply.

"Thank you for getting it all and some extra." She smiled as well as she could without hurting her check.

"Not a problem darlin'." He sat the box on the floor, watching her drop a few stuffed animals in it. He was happy to see her standing in the room, getting rid of things that brought about memories of Jerry. When she promised not to go back, he only half believed it. Watching her put things in a box for the trash confirmed she was done with him.

"If you waited for me though I would have left the key there too."

"I can take it to him." Nick snickered remembering the hospital.

"You don't need to go near him." She snapped back. He sounded a little too happy to go see Jerry. "I don't want to have to post your bail."

"I can post my own." This time she looked up from the boxes to see a heart-warming smile. Ornery, but a wonderful sight nonetheless.

She did not return the smile. "You promised to behave this morning."

"I promised not to kill him." Nick corrected her with complete sincerity.

"Nick!" She barked.

"That's more than once today you've used that tone with me."

"Sorry, it's a by-product of stress." She averted her eyes back to the box.

"It's not a bad tone. It's just not normal."

A wave of thankfulness swept over her because he didn't mind her newly acquired fiery spirit. She could feel his eyes searching her face. Not that he tried to hide it.

"I'm going to be watched for awhile. Aren't I?"

"Probably."

She didn't like the answer, but knew she would have to live with it. "You gonna let me drive tonight?"

"No, I will," He said, only considering the offer for a second before he answered. Nick knew her mind wouldn't be able to concentrate on the road. The drive would also do good for his stress level.

Kale walked through the doorway, grabbing Sonja's hand out of the box and pulling her close. "Do I smell better?"

"You almost smell human again." She chuckled as he tried to take a bite of her neck.

"Ready Nick?" Kale turned to see jealousy in his brother's eyes. Kale only smiled, hoping his brother wouldn't hit him right where he stood.

As they drove, Nick kept the radio on to distract her from thinking about Jerry. His heart floated as she sang under her breath and watched him drive.

Sonja couldn't help staring as Nick shifted through the gears and traffic. It was like watching a painter create a work of art. Each move smooth and effortless. She watched as he downshifted, pulling her eyes back to the road as he turned into a shopping center.

"What are we doing?" She questioned.

"You need furniture and this is the place to get it."

"I'm hungry," Kale piped in as his brother brought the car to a stop. It might have been useless to fight Nick, but after the long day he had, he was ready to eat. Another day of Sonja sleeping in Nick's bed wouldn't hurt anything.

Sonja stepped out of the car. Nick was right. They might as well get it over with.

"Help!"

She looked in the back seat to see Kale resembling a killer whale in a sardine can as he tried to pull himself out. She couldn't stop the laugh escaping as she offered her hand. "Are you having issues, Kale?"

Sweetly, she batted her eyes, tugging at his heart.

"Yes because my wonderful brother wouldn't let me drive." He almost pulled her into the back seat with him. Getting a stern look for his efforts.

After Nick decided they had enough fun laughing at him, he finally helped Kale out of the car.

When they were inside the store Nick asked for Marcus while Sonja looked confused, wondering if this was one of his stops this afternoon.

"Marcus this is our new roommate Sonja." Nick introduced her.

"It is a pleasure to finally meet you." His long hair swept back in a ponytail, his voice was smooth enough to melt ice as he kissed her hand.

"Likewise." Sonja caught herself unconsciously flirting until she realized Nick was standing next to her. She hid her face from him as she winced, waiting for the stern parental voice to sound. Then decided to speak before he could. "Marcus do you have the Romance Line?"

"I do." He looked at her with shock.

"She's an interior designer. She knows them all by heart." The tension returned to Nick's voice. Marcus was an old enough friend to know he shouldn't be flirting with Sonja.

"Do you have the sleigh bed in that line?"

"You are in great luck. I actually have one in queen size. I can have it delivered to you. Probably tomorrow."

"Wow, that would be great."

"Is the bed the only thing you need today?" He was still flirting with her in spite of Nick's looks.

"I think I want the entire set if you have it. If I remember right that would be a bed, dresser, two nightstands, a storage bench, and a desk."

"Good memory. You two want to see what she's talking about?" Marcus didn't wait for a response, offering his arm to Sonja, leading them all through the store. "Which finish Sonja?"

"Cherry."

"Good choice, it should match the floors in the Badeaux home perfectly."

"That's what I thought."

"Here it is."

Nick thought it was a beautiful set. The finish matched his own furniture as well as the hardwood floors. Their tastes being so alike never ceased to amaze him.

The brothers stood waiting while she paid for the furniture with her credit card. Kale's stomach growled, reminding them all they had not yet fed the bottomless pit. From the furniture store to the restaurant, Sonja continued to take jabs at the big man who couldn't get out of the tiny back seat she now occupied.

3.

They sat at a table in the bar and grill so the brothers wouldn't have to figure out who would sit next to Sonja. Instead they both did. The server brought the first round of drinks before anyone thought far into the food. Sonja started the night right. "A toast to no more Jerry. And hopefully a great living situation."

"Definitely drink to that." Kale added, as they all took a drink.

Sitting down the glass, she glanced around the dining area trying to figure out how to ask the question on her heart. Her eyes settled back on the table as the best wording formed, "I know it didn't take you that long from the time you each got home to clean out my apartment and get back to home."

They looked at each other, then smiled at her.

"How bad did it look?" Sonja crossed her arms in front of her on the table.

"We are both very proud of you," Kale piped up trying to get her to look him in the eyes.

"I'm not." She further averted her eyes, uncrossing her arms to play with the straw in her drink.

"You should be." Nick couldn't stay quiet. His fatherly tone was back.

"Why? Because I fell to his level. You all didn't. Did you?" She looked horrified, glancing from one to the other, at the thought of a few officers coming to the house to arrest them the first night she moved in.

"Neither of us laid a hand on him." Kale said truthfully.

"Don't. Just leave him be. Hold on, didn't lay a hand? What about feet, elbows and other body parts?" Sonja's voice cracked.

"Didn't touch him." Kale wasn't going to volunteer information about Nick yanking the call button out of Jerry's hand, let alone pushing the wires that held the man's legs up.

"Don't bother him again." When neither man said anything, she demanded, "Promise me."

Kale was the first to make eye contact with her. Perfectly seriously, he said, "If he doesn't come around then there will be no problems."

"Nick?"

Sonja tried looking him in the eyes as he took another drink and gazed across the room, but didn't answer. She couldn't force him to agree but she wanted at least what his brother could promise. The server brought another round of drinks, Sonja grabbed hers first and drained it.

"Sonja, I thought you quit drinkin'." Kale was astonished at the rate she slurped them down.

"Seems like that was an agreement against my will, and I think I deserve to get a little tipsy and have some fun."

"You make a lot of agreements don't you?" Nick caught his words too late. They were already out there. "Alright, no more for me tonight. I have to drive and already can't keep my foot out of my mouth."

Sonja couldn't help but laugh and smile as he passed his drink over to her.

They spent the rest of dinner laughing and talking about jobs, friends, and whatever else came up. Anything but Jerry.

37

As the meal wound down Sonja happily paid the bill. Standing for a restroom break she quickly found her bottom back in the seat. Nick caught her as she fell back, pushing her around in the chair so she would have something at her back. "Sonja?"

"Yeah Nick." She answered in a very breathy voice.

"You forgot it's been a long time since you drank, didn't you darlin'?" The smile that came across was sweet.

"Yep. And no one else decided to remind me either."

"You're the one that said you needed a little fun. Are you gonna get sick?"

"Na. Just don't think I can walk."

"Ready Kale?"

Nick slid each of her arms into her jacket as Kale finished his last drink. Together they helped her to stand slowly. Nick whispering, "Alright so far?"

"Yep."

They alternated steps so her feet would move with them.

Sonja couldn't help but laugh as her head rolled from one shoulder to the other all the way to the car.

Nick made sure Kale had a good hold on her as he let go and opened the car door.

As he rounded the front end to get in and try to help from that side, he heard someone yell, "Hey Nell."

He quickly looked around the parking lot to see a girl running over to another. He stuck his head in the car, "Be right back."

Kale looked past Sonja, very confused as his brother disappeared, grabbing Sonja as she slowly fell into the driver's seat. "You can't drive, don't think about it."

"Not like he would let me sober. It's his joy ride."

"You maybe. Me, no."

Nick crossed the drive, "Hey."

Each girl looked at him, then smiled. "Well, hello." One said.

"Sorry to stop you. Did I hear one of your names is Nell?"

"Yeah, I'm Nell." She said it very flirty, wondering who the good-looking guy was.

"Do you know a guy named Jerry Lane?"

Though her blond hair and blue eyes were the complete opposite of Sonja, she was still lovely.

"Yeah, he's in the hospital. Car wreck. You a friend of his?"

"Not really." Nick held his tongue trying to be nice. "But I think you need to meet my friend over here. If she's still conscience."

"Okay." She grabbed her friend's hand and followed Nick, glancing back to the other girl, who with the nod of her head agreed he was cute.

"Hey, Sonja?" He kneeled down so the two girls could look at Sonja through the door.

"Yes Nick." She said trying to match his deep voice, laughing at herself.

"There is someone here that knows Jerry that I think you need to met."

"Jerry is a jerk." She laughed again at the sounds mixing together.

"She's a little more toasted than even she realized." Kale said from where he stuck his head in from the back seat. "This the flower girl?"

"Yeah, she is." Nick said back. "Sonja, this is Nell. Have you met her before?"

"Nell. I don't know anyone with that name…

Oh… that's the name I found in Jerry's wallet last night."

"I'm sorry who are you?" Nell said from behind Nick, a little attitude in her voice. She wondered why this girl was going through her boyfriend's wallet.

"What? He didn't tell you he had a live-in girlfriend?" Sonja reached in her bag and pulled out a picture they had taken together, along with a few tissues. She handed Nick her wallet and started taking off the makeup as gently as her drunken hands would allow.

Nell showed the picture to her friend then handed it back. "So if you live with him why aren't you at the hospital with him instead of out with *two* other men."

Sonja finished taking off the makeup and sat up in the seat, turning toward the open door. Her head much clearer than before. She looked Nell straight in the eyes as she tilted her head to show the girl the bruises covering the left side of her face.

The bruises looked much worse than they had this morning. The outside was already starting to turn greenish-yellow while the inside stayed deep blue and purple, covering from just inside her ear to her temple, down to her jaw. Nick wanted to go back to the hospital and have security called on him, seeing where Jerry's knuckles pushed harder with nearly black indentions.

"I found your number in his wallet last night. I asked him if you were a friend from work. He got mad, said I had no right to look through his wallet. No right," She huffed "After over three years…" Sonja took a deep breath so she could continue. "Anyway, I explained it fell out when I picked up his pants to do laundry. He hit me for lying. Twice. That was before I could grab a lamp and hit him back. He wasn't in a car wreck. He got beat, by me, for three years of crap."

Sonja was shaking so badly that Nick grabbed her hands.

She was shaking because she didn't want the brothers to know exactly what happened. Maybe the alcohol pushed it out of her. Maybe the attitude from the girl. Maybe she just needed to get the poison out. She could see on Nick's face he wanted to kill Jerry. She was happy she couldn't see Kale. She answered with sad eyes, trying to get across an apology without saying it.

"I don't believe you. Jerry is such a nice guy."

The laugh escaping Sonja almost scared herself. "Nice guys don't hit women for asking about a phone number. Ask any nurse in the hospital why he is there or the cops that came to the apartment." Sonja sat back on the seat, "Nick I'm ready to go home when you are."

Nick shut the door as softly as he could.

Kale put his hand on her shoulder, "Sonja are you okay."

"I'll be fine Kale, thanks." She stared out the other side of the car from where they stood, hiding the bruises and trying not to look at the girl who helped cause them.

Outside the car, Nick explained to Nell about the flowers. About the nurse and about the last time Jerry hit Sonja. He also apologized that he had to be the one to tell her and for taking her time. He gave his number to her and explained that she should call if she had more questions—or any more problems with Jerry.

As the two girls walked away, Nick climbed in the driver's seat to find Sonja curled up in her seat fast asleep. His eyes ran across her face as he reached across and buckled her in.

"She fell asleep right after you shut the door."

41

Kale's voice softly came from the back seat.

"She's had a rough few days."

"The amount of alcohol she just consumed didn't help either."

"You remember what you were like when Donna left you?"

"Lets not start that." Kale had loved Donna, fully, totally. She left him two and a half years before. He found alcohol being the best way to drown the memories, and the pain. If not for the love of his brother and Sonja, he would probably still be somewhere stuck at the bottom of a bottle. When Kale's brain returned from memory lane he noticed they were half way home and he asked the question his brother couldn't. "How are we going to deal with this?"

That Nick still hadn't figured out. It wasn't the first time they had liked the same girl. It started in junior high and seemed to never stop. "We will let her figure it out when she's ready. If she even thinks that way about either of us."

When they arrived home Nick couldn't wake up Sonja—not that he tried too hard. After he laughed at his brother trying to get out of the back of his car, he carried her into the house. He carefully took her inside, laying her in his bed. Since she was asleep and couldn't object, he chose to take the couch for the night.

4.

The nightmare jolted Sonja from her deep sleep. Instead of finding herself lying in a hospital bed, she woke to the smell of Nick surrounding her. As her breathe returned to normal, she inhaled his scent. The smell of his cologne. His laundry soap. His shampoo. A slight hint of testosterone. Individually, each smell could belong to anyone. Mixed though, there was only one person on this earth with exactly that fragrance. It energized her, like airborne caffeine. She rolled toward the windows, knowing he put her there but chose not to join her. She understood why he didn't, though it disappointed her.

The alarm clock showed her it was only five in the morning, but her bladder screamed to get up. After the weight on her insides dissipated, she inspected her bruises in the mirror, hoping they would soon heal. Wandering out of the bedroom and down the stairs, she tried to straighten out her morning hair before opening the fridge to find a can of soda. The bad taste and sand paper in her mouth reminded her why she never liked to drink in the first place. She leaned against the kitchen island for several minutes with sleepy eyes, before noticing the back door standing wide open. Her heart pounded while she stepped slowly to the door afraid of what she might find.

The barn sat at an angle with the door facing the corner of the house so anyone could see in it from the kitchen window or the back porch. Through the morning fog, she could hardly see the targets Nick set up against the back fence. He stood perfectly in the middle of the two ancient oaks sending arrow after arrow into the targets, somewhere around seventy feet away. Even in the cool air, he didn't wear his coat. His hot nature kept him warm.

Nick owned the property, left to him by his grandparents. When he moved in, he insisted Kale move out of his cramped apartment and live with him on the farm. It was a beautiful piece of land. Almost five acres with farms on both sides. At some point, the family had owned it all. They sold off a little at a time to their neighbors as kids went to college and the family farmed less. The back of the property lined up with a long forgotten county road that only the farmers still used.

The brothers owned four horses at the moment. Without the land they wouldn't have that opportunity. It also gave them a large place to practice jousting, swordplay, and whatever else they wanted, like the archery at which Nick excelled. They belonged to several Renaissance organizations and groups. They enjoyed perfecting the ancient arts in their spare time, and she understood they would use those skills to keep her safe.

Deciding the cool morning air would finish the job of waking her up, she pushed the wooden framed screen door, and jumped a little as it slammed behind her. Nick still hit his mark and didn't turn around. "Hey Sonja."

"How'd you know it was me?"

"I saw the bathroom light in my room. Beside, Kale doesn't make loud noises when I have a weapon in my hand." He shot another arrow. Despite landing in the red bulls-eye, he looked disappointed.

"That would be smart on Kale's part," she said. "Probably not a good thing to do. You want to teach me how to use a sword or that thing."

Even without looking, he could see her waving her hand, a normal Sonja gesture that made him smile.

She added, "At least good enough to hurt the other guy and not me."

"We might be able to do that." Nick sent another arrow flying, still just missing the center.

He wasn't worried about hitting the target. Instead, he was trying to get out the frustration of her in his bed without him. He liked picturing Jerry as the target and her standing behind him was not helping either matter.

"Swords are easier than this 'thing'. Make sure the pointy end is away from you."

"Smart-aleck I know that much."

"Start with point and push."

The laugh poured out of her, as she took a seat on the stairs with her back against the wall of the house. Sipping the soda while Nick shot arrows, she noticed the sun coming up over the pine trees. There were so many things she loved about being here, being near the brothers was first on the long list. They made her feel good no matter how bad life got. These days life was so bad she took Friday off work. And she knew she could take more if she needed too. She would go back on Monday, now that she knew she could cover the bruises with makeup, had some place to sleep, and was safe from Jerry. Being away from work by itself drove her a little nuts. Almost two-and-a-half years, and Friday was the first day she took off. She had saved enough vacations to take three weeks and more if she needed.

What worried her now were hearts. Hers, Kale's, and most of all Nick's. She always knew they both liked her, not that it was any kind of secret. They both hated Jerry too. They just never knew they each had a place in her heart as well. At least not to the extent that they did.

She met Nick and Kale the first day of yet another dead end job while each of them was working through college. The job only lasted six months, but it became her favorite job because of the brothers. Sonja had been dating Jerry for six months, taking it slow, trying hard not to turn out like her sisters. Not to say her sisters weren't happy. It just wasn't the life for her, at least not with Jerry.

The only time she called on the brothers' love for her was the year before when Jerry hit her. They got in a fight. She slapped him first and he returned giving her a bloody nose and two black eyes. She had never hit anyone before but when he accused her of sleeping with her boss, something came over her. The brothers' love for her kept them from going after Jerry then. This time she would only ask and not say, "If you love me then don't."

When she found Nell's number she immediately knew it didn't belong to someone he worked with. It was a name and number written on a cocktail napkin. The shock of it set in and she didn't think twice about asking. She had to know and she found out all she need to—and more. Her stomach turned sour just thinking about how many other women he might have slept with while they were together. All of the suspicions she had were answered in that moment. She would make a doctors appointment to have her self checked out as soon as she could.

When Jerry hit her, she didn't feel it. Her brain shut down the pain while looking for a way to defend herself. It was the first time she ever wished she owned a gun, even though she was not entirely sure she would be able to pull the trigger and kill someone. A person's brain does odd things when pushed to extremes. When she finished kicking Jerry, she started moving. She placed the police call, knowing she didn't want to be alone when he regained consciousness. The ambulance took him away before he could wake up. She explained everything to the detective and officers that came in. Answered every question the best she could. She couldn't believe they sent a detective. He explained that her case was more violent than most and it was his job to see that hopefully it wouldn't happen again.

When the officers left she felt the pain in her face, took three aspirin and pulled boxes out from hiding under the bed. She had always known someday she would leave Jerry. She hoped it wouldn't be because he hit her. She had hoped she could find another way. Her contingency plan, whether he attacked her or not, was the same. At least it had been the same since shortly after the first time he was violent. She would pack and come to the brothers' farm, praying they would let her stay if only temporary, and hoping they would never have the heart to kick her out.

Unless she caused a fight between them. That was a worse nightmare than the one that woke her up that morning. The thought of putting any kind of wedge between the two of them broke her heart—more than finding Nell's phone number in the wallet, and much more than moving out of Jerry's apartment.

She had actually come close to running away with one of the brothers—Kale. She took him out after Donna left him. One of his favorite local bands was playing at a small club and she wanted to ease his pain. The music was great, the atmosphere was perfect.

When the band finished, the club deejay started more music. They danced for hours until he kissed her. It was passion mixed with a little love. When their lips separated, they took a minute of staring at each other then agreeing not to do that again. It wasn't bad. It caused her knees to go weak. Just wasn't right somehow, something inside told both of them that would be the closest they would ever come to the other. Neither ever told Nick.

She sat there staring at the view, both Nick and the sunrise, until the sun finished its morning ritual. Then she slipped back into the kitchen, careful not to slam the screen door since Nick was still armed and Kale was still asleep. Maybe after all her brain was getting better. She felt awful after talking to Nell. The alcohol wasn't having a good effect and the brothers heard much more from her about Jerry than she intended. Somehow, though, getting it out was uplifting.

As Sonja started breakfast, she watched Nick out the picture window moving around the barn feeding horses. She couldn't believe how much she enjoyed watching him work. His muscles actually showing through his shirt as he threw around the bags of feed. The gentleness of his hands rubbing the animals showed the love he held for them.

"I smell food."

The noise jolted her as Kale came in the kitchen still rubbing his eyes, his voice deep with sleep. She handed him a cup of coffee knowing how he liked it and pushed him back out the kitchen.

"Not nice Sonja."

"I'm cooking. You *don't* want to be in here." Sonja shook her head and then nodded it at the window. "How long will your brother be outside?"

"No clue. What is he doing?"

"Feeding horses."

"Why is he even awake?"

"Guessing the couch wasn't very comfortable. He was up before five."

Kale sat at the table, looking behind him to the couch, the bedding still on the end. The stack still folded the same as when they took it from the linen closet. His brother spent the night on guard, there was no question about it.

5.

Over breakfast, they discussed their chores. Each told her more than once that until they were sure Jerry wasn't going to come around they didn't want her outside unless one of them were as well. They also didn't like her staying at home without them but, as long as the doors stayed locked, Jerry wouldn't be a threat. Nick's fatherly tone was back and she felt like he was grounding her. Knowing he did it for her own good.

Only one road led to the farm, which dead-ended less than two miles down from their drive. If anyone came in or out the neighbors knew about it. Not saying the folks who lived nearby were nosy but Kale already explained the white Jetta would be at their home indefinitely.

Sonja ended up agreeing to do whatever chores the brothers didn't get to. She agreed knowing that for at least the first week she would have to settle in to the new room, house, and brothers. Her personal thoughts centered on making sure the boys didn't think they had to wait on her, that she was going to do her part.

As everyone finished nibbling on the leftovers from breakfast Sonja started clearing the plates off the table.

Nick jumped up. "I will take those."

"I can do the dishes." She quickly objected.

"You cooked. And I remember the last time you stayed here. You cleaned everything. We could eat off the floor, even in Kale's room. I would also like to keep the design on our grandmother's dishes a little longer."

"Fine, but you can't stop me from cleaning." The thought crossed more than once to start in Kale's room. She didn't tell him that. Cleaning was very therapeutic for her and she was sure even with how clean it looked neither of them had deep cleaned anything in the two years they lived there. Everything needed it from the last time she did it. She would have fun getting rid of the dirt. Her dirt as well as all the dirt in the house.

"Wouldn't dream of it, darlin'. Start in Kale's room." Nick laughed from the kitchen.

"I like my piles." Kale stated seriously, which normally he wasn't.

Ignoring Kale, she continued talking to Nick, "I figure if I stay home from work like the boss told me to on Monday, I could do that when Kale isn't here. Or I can do it when I get home from work."

"You stay out of my room." He still sounded serious as he stood, using his fists on the table to lean toward her, trying to intimidate her. His smile sort of ruined the effect. She matched his stance staring him down.

The loud knock on the front door stopped the discussion before either conceded the staring contest. She rounded the table laughing, heading for the door. Kale cut her off, wrapping his hand around her shoulders.

"Fine," she said. "I won't clean your room. Just the bathroom."

"I stopped you because you aren't answering doors for a while."

"You have got to be joking." Sonja rolled her eyes looking up at him.

"Dead serious." Came from the kitchen over the running water.

Kale jogged across the living room smiling because he won the first argument over his room, and knowing she would clean it anyway. He opened the door to find two men and a box spring on the front porch.

"See? It was for me anyway. Nick you get your bed back tonight!" Sonja called.

"Not like I will sleep anyway," came from under his breath. He didn't try the night before because he had too much pent up anger, still wanting to make Jerry pay somehow. Not to mention that he wanted to climb into bed with Sonja and tell her what he felt. He was just now starting to pay the price for the lack of sleep. He would sleep for a bit and leave Kale in charge. Then stay up again tonight.

Kale directed the movers how to maneuver the furniture up the L shaped staircase without breaking anything, then down the hallway. When the movers finished, they enjoyed a large glass of ice tea before they were on their way.

Kale helped Sonja make her new sleigh bed and move her things around in the room. He loved spending time with her. They talked about anything and everything. She was the only female he ever knew that he could do that with. The only one he dared to tell his deepest thoughts. She knew more about him than probably his own brother. Kale sensed something about her that told him—and anyone else whom she let close—any secret was safe with her. She would keep it and never throw it back in your face.

When Donna left him, Sonja was the one who helped him the most through the heartache. At least as much as she could. She listened. She empathized. She was exactly what he needed when he needed her. It was the final straw in unleashing his feelings toward her. Then came the kiss that made it apparent to them both it would never be more. Again, he had Sonja and Nick to thank for getting him out of two weeks of self-loathing. They came in his apartment after a good night of drowning his sorrows, slid his hung over body in the bathtub, and flipped on the cold shower. Nick kept him in the tub by force as Sonja explained to him that they weren't going to let him treat himself like this over anyone. It was the closest he ever came to landing a fist on his brother in real rage. The closest he came to throwing Jerry back in Sonja's face. He was thankful later that he didn't follow through with either.

He didn't doubt that she harbored some kind of feeling for him even after their agreement about the kiss, but he could see what she felt for Nick was more. What Nick felt for her was more as well. He would just run interference until he was sure that Sonja was ready to start a new relationship with Nick. Save her from herself and from his brother.

He left her to finish moving in so he could go brush down horses. On the way out the door, Nick informed him he was going to sleep for a while with the door open so if anything happened he would know. Kale watched the road, driveway, and trees while he cleaned and brushed the horses.

When Sonja finished emptying the boxes, she flattened and slid them under the bed. She thought for a moment about cleaning then decided fresh air would do her good. As she stepped out the screen door, she found Kale walking the horses around the backyard and decided to ask if she could take one out to the backfield.

"Not by yourself, you won't." Kale almost

glared at her over the back of Orion.

"What? You want to throw around orders like your brother now?"

"I'll go out with you. I'm not throwing around orders. . . just following them." He pulled a saddle off the wall and threw it over Orion's back. "Let me show you how to do this."

He walked through the motions. He straightened the horse blanket first, then buckled the strap underneath. He sat a crate on the floor and helped her push into the saddle before sliding in behind her. The closeness of their bodies would drive him insane but he could see no other way. He steered the enormous animal to the wall, pulling down a practice sword. Sonja's eyes questioned him, worry lining her brow.

"If I didn't Nick would shoot me." He steered the horse out of the barn heading for the back pasture.

"I have caused him a little of stress over the past few days." Sonja looked at the sword wondering when Nick would teach her to use one.

"A little? More like ready to bust at the seams."

"Maybe I should find an apartment sooner rather than later."

"No, then he would sleep in his car outside your apartment building and drive us both even more insane. He has every right to be concerned. We both do. He's just a little over the top."

"That's one of the things I like about him," she smiled, leaning against Kale's shoulder, "he's serious with a fun side. You are fun with an ever so small serious side. Kinda like a yin yang. You balance each other nicely."

"Not when we were kids."

She sighed and waited, since she loved to hear stories about them.

"Fought like rivaling brothers." He played it up to be dramatic. "If you could believe that. Now we save up our anger and beat on each other with swords. It's very healthy. Like you and cleaning."

With the boys being only twenty months apart, she could imagine the fireworks between them. Her own sisters had their fair share of catfights and there were almost three years between each of the four of them.

"Nick said he might teach me to use a sword. Who knows maybe I'll *like* it." She looked very pleased at the thought.

"If you like it, Jerry is in for more pain than me or Nick could cause him."

His heart pounded when Sonja laughed.

Nick dreamt of running Jerry through with one of his swords. It was very satisfying, but too quick. He wanted the man to suffer, to rip off his limbs, and beat him with them.

He also dreamt of her as many times before. The dream never went well, a few times he poured his heart out to her, and she laughed. Other times she said it was Kale she loved. Yet other times she went running back to Jerry. In those dreams where he didn't tell her how he felt, they both ended up alone for eternity.

He woke in a cold sweat. The dream still went wrong. He crawled out of bed heading for the shower, trying to wash away the dread.

When he was dressed he went to find her. Her room was already perfect, everything put away and the boxes gone. He admired the room because it screamed Sonja. Her bed was set cattycorner between the two double windows so either way she would get sunlight, moonlight, and moving air when the windows were open. Her dresser sat across the room by the closet, the desk close to the western window where she could use her computer and watch any sunsets that happened by, as well as the driveway.

Candles lined most of the furniture tops, the orchids he brought her on the nightstand by her bed and pictures of her nieces and nephews everywhere. He would get a new rug for the center of the room and add to her small collection of accessories, whether she wanted him to or not.

He left the upstairs to find the rest of the house empty. When she wasn't in her room, his stomach ached a tad. Now it was in full knots. He grabbed the bow and arrows out of the mud closet by the back door and went to find them.

The backyard was empty. The cars were in the driveway. His pulse raced. Someone could have come in while he was in the shower and he would have never known it. They could've been outside and gone in a flash. He ran to the barn finding Kale's horse gone, deciding he was going to shoot his brother, he headed toward the back of the property.

Sonja and Kale trotted around the pasture for almost thirty minutes, talking away. She could see the trail where they normally rode compared to the tall grass around the outside of the pasture. Orion was strong and took the two of them on his back well.

An arrow whizzing past to a tree stopped their ride. Sonja almost screamed until she realized what it was and where it came from. Her initial reaction told her she was stressed herself.

"Think we're in trouble little sister. What do you think?"

"Think we better ride that way before he shoots

another one."

6.

By the time Kale paced his horse back to the outer perimeter of the pasture Nick was fuming. "I was worried sick. What do you think your doing running all over the place with the possibility that Jerry might come around."

"Quit yelling at your brother." She slid down from the saddle. "I asked him if I could ride. He said not alone. He took a sword and all." She already felt like she was pushing them apart, and she arrived just over twenty-four hours ago. "The detective is going to call me before Jerry is released, anyway."

Nick's heart slowly melted with each second that her eyes showed their fire. "Sound like an old hen, don't I?"

"More like the father I lived without." She headed into the house in a huff. She didn't need to be scolded. She needed her friends, and she needed their love.

When Sonja was out of ear's reach Kale started in, "Great move, Nick."

"Me? You are the one taking her away from the house."

"Like she said, he's in the hospital and I was armed." Kale eyed his brother with bad intent as Nick marched into the barn. He returned with another sword before Kale could continue.

"You want to work out that frustration, or do

you think you are going to beat me when you're mad?"

"Yes." They both smiled as Nick mimicked Sonja's habit of answering both questions with one word.

Kale pulled his sword from its sheath that they had attached to the saddle for competition and they squared off.

Like any girl who had been told by her father she couldn't do what she wanted, Sonja wanted to slam the door as she went in. Instead, she pulled a beer out of the fridge, taking half of it in one swallow. He wasn't her father and wasn't her lover, but a friend so dear that she cared in the deepest part of herself about his emotions. Several deep breaths later, leaning against the island that she wanted to actually strike with a fist, she reminded herself she didn't want to be temperamental. While still trying to talk herself out of descending into an alcohol induced coma, she heard the sound of metal against metal coming from the backyard. Looking out the back porch, she considered yelling at them or picking a side and cheering. Remembering what Kale told her about them taking out their frustrations that way she figured it was good for them. Maybe even good for her.

She dropped the beer bottle in the trash before letting the back screen slam behind her as she went out, stomping down the stairs she double checked that she had their attention. Before walking straight through the middle of them on her way to the barn.

"Where are you going?" Nick watched as she trudged along, his brother almost catching him with lucky shot while he was distracted. "No fair."

"Let her be." Kale called as he swung again.

They both turned as she came back out of the barn with a sword in each hand. "Which one?" she asked in a tone a little more chipper than her body language expressed.

Nick shot her a look of "Don't". "Neither. You don't know how to use one."

Kale tried another swing on his brother. Which he saw from the corner of his eye and deflected.

Sonja turned her attention to Kale. He smiled as he said, "The one on the left."

She turned back to the barn putting away the sword in her right hand. She was beginning to fear that she might have lost the last bit of sanity she had.

When she came back out of the barn, Nick threw his opinion at her again. "Now go put that one back too. Kale don't encourage her."

"Take a swing at him. You will feel better." Kale said ducking his brother sword.

Sonja pointed the sword at Nick trying her best to look mean. Her blood was boiling, she was so mad at him. Still she didn't think she could hit either of them. She saved that for people who hit her.

She swung, he pushed the blade to the ground with his, leaving the two of them face to face.

"If you are that worried about *my* safety then teach me. Otherwise, you can take your fatherly concern and shove it."

Her brown eyes didn't waiver. She smelled like vanilla and horses, neither of which was unpleasant on her. Nick pulled the sword from her hands, walking almost to the back porch before he stuck it in the ground and half turned back to her.

She refused to back down. If he wanted to play daddy, or knight in shining armor, instead of seeing her point, she would have to push harder. She lifted her head, huffed, and turned back to the barn. She was trying her hardest to act like a spoiled brat.

"Come here Sonja." Nick sounded defeated despite his fatherly tone. After all, he did want her to be able to defend herself. The bruises that she chose not to cover today were a harsh reminder of how much she needed to be able to protect herself against anyone.

Stopping, she slowly turned around to find Nick looking at the ground. She glanced out the corner of her eye to see Kale leaning against the closest ancient oak, wishing he would jump in with something constructive—or at least tell her to stop pushing.

When she didn't step toward him Nick decided he needed to concede a little more. "I suggest you come here before I change my mind."

Carefully she came toward him. He was still armed and fuming. She could hardly breathe as he stepped behind her, wrapped his arms around her, and put the sword firmly in both hands. "You need to keep a firm grip. No one should be able to pull the sword from your hands."

She tightened her grip. He loosened his. "You need to move from the wrists not the shoulders and elbows." He manipulated her wrists, turning the sword around several times for her to get the feel for the weight of the weapon.

His breath down her neck and him whispering in her ear made her arms weak but she held firm to the sword. She didn't want the "father" type back, at least not with him so close. His hands over hers felt good. Felt right. She tried keeping her breath steady, happy he was behind her and couldn't see her face.

He turned her body, sounding happier, "Want to try to hit Kale?"

Kale watched closely, the look on Sonja's face told him everything he needed to know. She was frightened and not by Jerry but by his brother—and not of his anger or any physical threat from the sword—but by his being that close to her, touching her.

Sonja answered before Kale could. "After the way you've acted since you woke I'd rather take a few more at you."

"Sorry about that but I was worried. My brother and best friend disappear while I'm asleep. There were endless possibilities."

"You didn't sleep last night did you?"

"None of your concern. Now hold firm. Kale take a swing and try to hit the blade so she can feel the vibrations."

Kale was still leaning against the oak pondering the next move. This one was going far better than he could have hoped. A little more pushing his brother and Sonja would know exactly how Nick felt about her.

He stepped up and took a light swing at her, she dropped the sword as it vibrated. Nick pulled his arms off her, ran his hands through his hair, and looked at sky as she picked back up the sword and tightened her grip.

"Again."

Kale met her eyes and, finding them determined, glanced at his brother, who couldn't look. He swung. Again, she dropped it.

She picked it up and took her stance. She didn't flinch as Nick wrapped his arms around hers with his hands gliding down on top of hers. He whispered softly. "You are too afraid that Kale is going to hurt you."

Whispering back, as her heart hammered, "Maybe a little."

"He won't. You know that deep down. Just hold tight." He looked at his brother and nodded.

Kale took a swing and hit the blade. The vibrations coursed through her body but she smiled when the sword didn't fall to the ground. Even more determined she said, "Again."

Nick nodded. Kale swung and she grimaced as it rocketed through her body. "Now loosen your elbows and shoulders. Only your fingers should be that tight to keep a hold of it."

Sonja found it hard to loosen up with Nick wrapped around her. She took a deep breath, "Again."

This time the hit didn't vibrate as bad as she smiled at Kale. He swung again. Nick began moving her wrist so she could meet the swings. That made the sword vibrate even less, though a quake was starting in the center of her stomach. Nick was touching her. His hands moved smoothly over her arms. The pushing, to make her body do what he wanted, was gentle. He slowly moved his hand up her arms, giving her more and more control as Kale took each swing.

As they moved back and forth over it, Sonja understood why this part of the backyard wouldn't grow grass.

When Nick ran out of arm he put his hands on her hips, so if anything went wrong he could move her from Kale's sword. It might have only been a practice sword but it was still sharp and heavy enough to hurt. They danced in this way for an hour as she improved with each swing.

"Alright I'm done." Kale finally sighed handing his sword to Nick as he went inside.

Nick looked at Sonja questioning if she wanted to spar with him. The look said she was terrified. "Remember you can't be scared and use a sword."

"I'm not afraid of you with that."

"Really?" He smiled, wondering how ornery he could be. Then chose to take a swipe at her. She deflected it perfectly as if he was still behind her guiding her body.

"Should I be?" She sidestepped to keep him in front of her.

"Never." He took another swing. Nick saw her grimace as the blow vibrated through her body. He was distracting her from concentrating. "Loosen up."

"Easier said than done."

"Do I need to take it way from you?"

"Try." The smile was back on her face with a good amount of fire in her eyes.

He stepped forward, put the tip of the swords against the ground and his body against hers, and then pulled as the sword slipped from her fingers, never losing sight of her eyes.

"Now you are too loose."

"I'll have to try harder next time." She had no idea what else to say. He was pushing every button and pushing them right. He handed back the sword and went back to a safe distance waiting for her to take her stance, then swung.

Kale left Sonja and Nick striking at each other while he started dinner. He watched through the back door as they laughed. A few more plans and they would be in each other's beds, at least as long as they didn't concern themselves with him. That is where the trick came in for him. He needed to find some way to let them each know that he would stop them without hurting anyone—and not until he was sure Sonja was ready for the next step in her life.

Sonja's face was serious. She didn't take any of the sword fighting directions as a joke. She would use a sword if someone forced her to defend herself. Everything in her said Jerry would be back, he would try his best to take her from the brothers.

Nick again took the dishes away from Sonja after dinner, this time pointing out the beautiful flowered pattern on them as he went to the kitchen.

Sonja went up the stairs to a hot bath. Her muscles hurt from swinging the weapon for several hours and she smelled from the horses. She lit a few candles as the bubbles filled the claw-footed bathtub.

She pulled the window drapes closed as she stepped into the steaming water, with a pad and pen. She needed to make a list of the things she considered necessary for her new room and bathroom. The water felt good as she slid down. Felt good on her bruised face especially.

After she finished in the tub she watched as the water went down the drain, too relaxed to move just yet. When she finally dragged herself out, she wrapped her hair in the towel. She realized she needed to add a bathrobe to her list. She poked her head out of the bathroom and jumped across to her room. Slipping into her favorite pair of light green pajamas, she headed downstairs.

The house was empty. She slipped on her sneakers at the back door as she went out, not letting the screen door slam this time. The lights from the back corners of the house and from the barn lit up most of the backyard.

Kale's horse was back in his stall and the swords were no longer on the back porch. She saw each brother holding a bow pointed at a target. She sat quietly on the porch, letting her legs hang over the edge, watching attentively. From where she sat, most people wouldn't be able to tell one from the other. The forms matched with the muscles in their arms and backs taunt as the bows were bent to their capacity. She knew which of the brothers was which even though they weren't facing her. Nick was a little taller, a little bigger. And he had been pulling on her heart all day. Having him so close when he was showing her how to use the sword drove her hormones insane. She wanted to ask about the bow but she wasn't sure she could take the close quarters again so soon.

Kale on the other hand she could stand to be that close to. It was like having a very attractive stepbrother. It's wrong but not legally wrong to find him attractive. She understood how much fun they would have together, but sooner or later they would drive the other insane. She was overly clean. He was overly messy. He rarely took anything seriously. She needed a little seriousness.

Nick on the other hand was clean, without being as anal about it as she was. He was normally serious but could joke, like he did about her scrubbing the dishes so clean she would actually remove the designs. Anyway she hoped it was a joke. The best thing right now was they each loved her at some level and would protect her if Jerry were actually stupid enough to come around. She watched as another arrow hit the mark, hoping Jerry wasn't that stupid. She wanted to rip him limb from limb but she didn't want the boys to kill the guy, or anyone, in her honor.

"Are you just gonna sit up there or do you want to learn this too?" Nick didn't turn around.

Kale glanced her way, "How long you been up there?"

"About five arrows." She said getting up, bouncing down the stairs and across the yard to where Nick was waiting. He handed the bow to her putting her hands in the proper places.

"Pull it back." She pulled. All the muscles were pulling but the bow wasn't moving.

"Keep trying." Nick said with actual encouragement in his voice as he walked to the house and disappeared inside. He came back out with the six-pack of beer in hand. "Someone's been in this already." He handed one to his brother and started nursing his own.

"What about me?" Sonja asked with a slight pout.

"After last night you don't need any. Keep pulling."

"I'll keep pulling, but if I do figure out how to use this you're in trouble." Gritting her teeth, trying harder to pull.

Nick's eyes flash a moment of orneriness as he spoke, "Scared! You? Kale?"

"Very." He shook his head, "Especially if she puts on boots and starts kicking ribs."

She pulled again, the bow sprang open. "Wow there's a point at which it gives."

"That's called 'breaking over.'" Nick took another drink. "Let go and do it again."

Watching her try was as entertaining as torturous. She let it go, the string hit her thumb. She dropped the bow and stuck her thumb in her mouth.

"Now you know not to let it go like that, you can have the beer." Nick popped the top off and handed it to her, she yanked it out of his hand, pulled the thumb she was nursing out and took a good drink.

She could see he felt bad about it but was also trying to hold back the laughter. He bent down to pick up the bow and she kicked him in the butt. "Pay back. You knew it would snap back like that."

"Yes I did but you wanted to learn and that's the best way to learn not to let go like that." He wanted to take the thumb and suck on it himself. He resisted that urge along with so many others.

They spent the rest of the night outside sitting on the picnic table, talking, joking, and being friends while she continued to try to figure out the bow.

Her body was warm against his as Nick wrapped his arms around her, under the sun. He leveled the bow to her height, "Look down the arrow and line it up with the red part of the target."

His whispers were causing her eyes to blur, making the target almost impossible to see. Sunday was playing out a lot like the day before.

"Hold it there until you are sure, then let go."

Letting go. There was a thought to make her mind move. She took a deep breath trying to concentrate on the red dot so far away. *Letting go,* she could drop the bow, turn and kiss him and shock him. He in turn would either kiss her back, which would probably lead to a very embarrassing display in front of Kale no less. Or push her away.

Nick noticed her body showed confidence, but her eyes showed fear. He kept asking himself why. She was becoming proficient enough with the weapons that they didn't scare her anymore. He had to assume that it was him.

She couldn't shake the feeling that Jerry was coming after her, that she couldn't escape him. Added to the fact that Nick stayed close to her all day, driving her wild, she was a bundle of nerves. His teaching didn't make her nervous but his body did. His muscles stretched around her, holding her safe.

The arrow sailed through the air landing in the red. Sonja beamed at Nick when she turned.

"Not to shabby, darlin'. Do it again." He wrapped his arms back around her as she took her stance, hoping she would want to do this all day.

Sonja chose to cook dinner for them, even with how sore her muscles were it gave her a few minutes without being incased in Nick's body. At least after all these years she understood how they stayed in perfect shape. It wouldn't take them long to have her that way too. Her cell phone rang, for the first time since Friday, she looked at it as if it would bite before picking it up.

"Hello?"

"Hello, Ms. Mitchell?"

"Yes, can I help you?"

"This is Detective Ivan, I told you I would call when Mr. Lane was released."

"Yes, Detective. Thank you. When?" She glanced out the window to see the brothers cleaning up outside, far from being able to listen to her on the phone.

"About twenty minutes ago. His mom paid his bail so we had no choice. The judge is going to see him again in six weeks for the charges. April twenty-eighth is the date I have here. Until then you should be okay. Depends on the judge what happens from that point. I wouldn't go down any dark alleys alone, though. Does he know where you are staying?"

"Maybe, maybe not. If he thinks about it I'm sure he can figure it out. But I have two men here that won't let him get near the house."

"Nice to have friends like that."

"Very." She rested her head on the island. Thoughts of Jerry coming to the house and the mayhem that would cause churning her stomach.

"Well I need to make a few more phone calls. Call me if you need any help with that guy."

"I definitely will Detective, thank you."

She hung up the phone, stirring the rice for

dinner. Now she just needed to figure out if she should tell the boys. They needed to know in order to be on the look out, but after yesterday with Nick, she wasn't sure if he could handle more. She was afraid if he knew he would lock her in her room. Or his. And not let her out.

She was still contemplating what to do as Nick and Kale came through the back door. She tried to look busy setting the table and avoid their eyes.

"What's wrong? What don't you want to tell us?" Nick never missed a beat, whether it was her body language, or a sixth sense.

"I hate it when you do that." She glared at him through the archway.

"That's not the answer to the question." He grabbed her arm as she tried to pass him then her chin, careful not to push anything that might still be bruised. He stared in her eyes then wrapped his arms around her. "When did they let him go?"

That he knew her so well almost made her cry. "About thirty minutes ago."

When Nick let go of her she tried to head to the kitchen to get dinner. Kale grabbed and hugged her, and this time the tears began to fall. She couldn't help it. She was scared. She might be able to play strong for Nick, but not for Kale. She couldn't. He never lied to her and never held back anything—other than maybe what he felt inside for her—though that might come at some point.

Nick left the room. She hit Kale in the chest, at least as much as she could with him pressed against her.

"Sonja, he won't get near you."

She shook her head, understanding he was right. Knowing she was safe. "You made me cry."

"Sorry. You looked like you needed it."

Nick locked the front and back doors, then

checked that all the windows were secure. Kale kept her in his arms until she finished crying. When he finally let her go, setting her in a chair, he put dinner on the table. Nick washed his hands in his bathroom and grabbed his set of small knifes off the dresser before returning to the dining room.

They ate in silence. When everyone finished, Kale took the hint from his brother and began clearing dishes. Nick pulled out the black case and opened it. "Pick one or two."

Sonja looked in the case. "No."

"Why not?"

"I would be more afraid of hurting you or Kale than getting Jerry with one."

"Would me or Kale come inching in your room at night?"

He wasn't saying he hadn't thought about it the night before, or wouldn't ever think about it again. He wouldn't inch in, he would open the door turn on the light and tell her everything. He wouldn't jump on her in her bed with no warning.

A needed laugh escaped from Sonja at the thought of one of them sneaking into her room. "No. Well you might not. Kale? Who knows. . . "

"Heard that." Echoed out of the kitchen.

"Can you deny it?" She yelled but nothing came back.

"Take one. You will make me sleep better." Sonja closed her eyes, rolling her head. She knew that for two nights he hadn't slept well, if at all. She pulled out a knife. He pulled out the matching one and placed it beside her before zipping up the case.

"I don't need two."

"You have two hands. I am going to bed." He gave her a kiss before he thought about what he was doing. Then he turned and went up the stairs as slowly as he could without giving away his sudden recognition that he shouldn't have done that.

Kale came out of the kitchen. She was still staring at the stairs Nick had ascended. Kale leaned over her shoulder, whispering in her ear, knowing the timing was right. "He loves you."

"I know." She could hardly hear her own voice.

"I don't think you fully do." When she turned to meet his eyes, he said, "You know it's different."

She understood and refused to hurt anyone. She smiled, kissed his forehead, "Night brother."

"Night, sister."

Sonja put the blades on her new nightstand and curled up in bed. Her last thought as she drifted way, Nick.

Sonja woke at two this time with the same dream of the hospital. It caused her chest to ache. Nick had tried to defend her and lost completely and Kale was in the hospital bed next to her. Even though her mind assured her that unless Jerry shot them from a great distance, they would never be hurt that way, and that was something he could never do. Her heart still pounded. The tears still poured from her.

When she regained control again, she wandered through the dark, one of the knives in her hand. Kale's door lay open, she peered in to see him sleeping soundly. Nick's door lay open as well, he was not sleeping, at least not in his bed.

She crept down the stairs as quiet as she could to see the couch was empty. The front and back doors were locked, the front porch empty, the back porch and yard empty too. She drank almost an entire glass of tea before she started back up the stairs to find her cell phone and call his. She was still scratching her head when she stepped into her room. He grabbed her from behind, his hand over her mouth before she had a chance to scream, the knife dropped to the floor.

He had watched as she sat up in bed very upset. He wanted to console her but thought better than to inch in her room. She hadn't seen him as she left her room, a knife in her hand. He had waited for her to come back.

"See now you should have had that knife in my arm before I could say or do anything."

She didn't know if she wanted to kill or hug him as he let go of her. She turned, burying her head in his bare shoulder and cried instead. Between the dream and the fact she couldn't find him in the house, she couldn't hold it in anymore. Crying was becoming a bad habit she wanted to stop. She couldn't remember crying so much in her life as she had since entering this house. This time she couldn't stop it. Earlier she hadn't let him see her cry, too worried that it would push him further off the deep end.

"Sonja! I'm so sorry I didn't mean to scare you." He hugged harder.

She shook her head no, but could not speak to tell him why she was crying between sobs.

He slowly backed her into her bedroom, sitting her on the storage bench at the end of the bed. He knelt in front of her, trying to get her to look at him as he dried her tears with his thumbs.

"Please, don't cry."

He could hear the desperation in his own voice. His heart breaking, he wanted to kiss away the tears. This time he was happy he thought and chose not to act. One kiss for the day was enough.

Once she stopped crying enough to speak, she

wanted to scream at him. The look on his face pulled on her heart so she didn't. She could see the love in his eyes. She wasn't prepared for how deeply the look would affect her. His face changed.

"You okay, darlin'?" Came out as a half throat clear.

"Yeah Nick. What are you doing awake?"

"Couldn't sleep. You?"

"Nightmare."

"Same one that woke you yesterday?"

"Worse."

"Where were you hiding?" The edge was starting to come back to her voice.

"I wasn't hiding, just watching your room from the library."

"Go to bed you'll hear me scream if anything happens."

"You didn't scream when I grabbed you."

"I knew it was you as soon as you touched me." She wanted to add more, his smell, his breath, his stare, but she knew it would only lead to heartache at this point. Most likely his.

"Not to mention, Jerry isn't you." Never was, she was just too blind to see it. She crawled across her bed and snuggled under the covers, not wanting him to see the regret in her eyes.

"I'm not worried about Jerry." He walked out the door.

"Good night, Nick."

"Good night, darlin'." Echoed down the hall.

7.

Monday morning came early for everyone. Kale crawled out of bed first to jump in the shower. Nick stayed curled up until his brother shut off the water, enjoying the dreams of Sonja that for once went well. Then he went in the shower. He waited every morning so he could have a hot shower instead of splitting the water pressure between two.

Sonja jumped out of bed when her brain registered that the clock said six. She went straight for the make up and hair, happy she took her bath the night before. Nick and Sonja almost ran into each other at the point the hallway connected. He let her go first watching as she bounced down the stairs in front of him. Kale already had the house smelling of biscuits and eggs. Sonja threw together a sandwich, and started out the door.

"See you two after work." She threw out as she grabbed her jacket.

"Stop right there." Nick's fatherly voice was back.

"What? I don't remember how long it will take to get to work from here and I don't want to be late after missing Friday."

"I'll drive you." Kale piped in, pushing food in his mouth.

"I'll pick you up." Nick added.

"I can drive myself, you know I have for several years."

"It's not the drivin' we're concerned about."

Kale continued to eat knowing he had a minute while they exchanged opinions again.

She crossed her arms, "I arrive every day at the same time, with seven other people. I leave the same time with those seven people. I go to lunch with one to five of them every day."

"I still don't like it." Nick said without a smile on his face. He watched as Sonja pulled one of the knives out of her back pocket.

"Satisfied?"

"Impressed, but no."

"Kale will follow you, I will meet you there tonight." He decided to compromise as she became more agitated.

"Whatever makes you happy. Ready Kaleb?"

"Ouch! Full name. See ya later, bro." Kale pushed one more bite and followed her out the door.

Nick didn't like it but it would have to do.

Sonja walked in the front doors of J and D Design as Kale pulled away, honking, and waving. Since she was still fuming, she didn't wave back. The building was modern with the entire front made of glass. The showroom displayed previous projects, interior and exterior.

The office consisted of Jack, the J of J and D Design. D, Diane had divorced him a few months before Sonja started and never came in. Sonja wasn't sure if she still owned part of the company and chose not to come in, or if Jack owned it solely.

Linda the receptionist was already at the front desk. She was bubbly and interacted well with the clients. Her blonde hair and blue eyes attracted more men to stay in the showroom until someone could help them. Since Linda was the newest employee of eight months, Sonja knew the least about her. Linda was good at her job, something Sonja appreciated even if she didn't like her personally.

"Messages?"

"Tons." Linda let out a little exasperated, her tone changing quickly. "How you doing Sonja?"

"Alive and kicking. Ready to put my head in someone's house." Sonja wasn't going to explain she meant literally. She was just furious at men in general. "Mrs. Roland mad?"

"Layla did the presentation perfect. The lady went out of here smiling, saying you are brilliant."

"Would have liked to have seen that." The Roland project had been a thorn in her side for roughly six months. Mrs. Roland changed her mind five times a day instead of letting Sonja do her job. Finally, three weeks ago Sonja told Mrs. Roland she was doing the interior if she didn't like it she could take her money elsewhere. It was the beginning of what Sonja considered the emergence of her fiery new self.

"Make sure Jerry Lane doesn't get through to me. If he calls twice, tell him I will get a restraining order. Fourth time transfer to me, with a warning, and he can talk straight to my lawyer."

"That bad?"

"Yeah that bad. Layla and Jack in already?" Sonja headed toward the offices.

"In your office waiting."

"Longer drive than usual. Thanks Linda."

Sonja ended the conversation when she was already half way down the hall. All the messages were from clients. Now she just had to deal with the others in the office before she could dig down to her work. It was time to put her mind on something, anything other than

Jerry, or even Nick.

Each person worked in her or his own private office, other than Linda. Jack was the only one who had a key to every office. When she walked in, everyone was in hers.

Brad stood in the doorway, he was a nice guy all five feet eight inches took up the doorway with two hundred and fifty pounds. He and Melanie did the architectural designs for the company. Melanie was standing next to Sonja's filing cabinet. Sonja always thought she was a backstabber. It was something about the way she acted. Ann was standing next to the other wall, happy to see Sonja. Ann reminded her of what her mother should have been like. A working mom with kids who always came first, as long as it didn't kill her. She did the accounting for the company. In the beginning, she and Sonja had exchanged words about the cost of projects. Ann soon learned Sonja knew what she was doing and wasn't some snot-nosed kid. Phyllis was the oldest of the company, she did the purchasing from the numerous companies they dealt with. No one could say anything bad about her, she was the sexy grandmother type and loved everyone. Phyllis sat in the visitor chairs with Layla.

Layla was the closest thing Sonja had to a friend other than the brothers. Jack was a friend too, but still her boss. Layla only stood 5' 4" with sandy hair and big green eyes. They met when she hired Layla on her first interview. Layla had impressed her with her work ethic, honesty, and experience. They went shopping every now and again, and enjoyed lunch together almost daily. She and Sonja were the decorating part of their little team. Everyone reported to Sonja in some way and she to Jack. He sat in her chair on the other side of her desk. He was a handsome man with salt and pepper hair. Sonja was sure he was a hippie in his day, at least that's what his mannerism said about him.

"Sorry I'm late, Jack. Did I miss anything?"

Sonja was always business, a fact no one else ever forgot because she wouldn't let them. She had no doubt, though, that she was the talk of the small office on Friday. It was the first day she had missed in her entire time with the company.

"Did Linda tell you about the Roland project?"

"Said the lady went out happy. That's what we do right." She wasn't pushing Jack out of her seat but she was already working around him, while they spoke.

"Sonja should you even be here today?"

Sonja stopped setting her things up in order to look around the room at her coworkers. As the boss—well the boss minus Jack—she should explain some of what happened to her. Layla's face implored her to talk about something other than work.

"For the record, I am fine. Thursday night Jerry and I got in a fight. I moved out on Friday and in with a few old friends. Jerry was released from the hospital yesterday. It is either sit in an empty house all day or work my tail off. If I sit at home I would clean it from top to bottom, again I can do that here."

"Then lets get to work." Jack jumped to her rescue.

"Thank you. I also need to look for a new rug for my bedroom."

"We have plenty." Jack was already writing it off as a bonus. "Furniture?"

"Delivered on Saturday."

"Never waste time do you?" He waited until only he and Layla were left in the office with her then shut the door. "Now really how are you?"

"Fine, Jack I promise." She couldn't help but

talk more softly. He was a friend and a wonderful boss, with nothing but concern for her.

"Then why do you have a knife in your back pocket?"

"To make my roommates happy. And one still followed me to work. They're afraid that Jerry might try and show up."

"Is it Kale and Nick?" Layla leaned forward as if it was juicy gossip.

"Yes, it is."

She had spent most of her live keeping people away. Never having a father was one of the reasons. Watching her mother work away her life didn't help. Her sisters giving up their lives for men, for love, was probably the last straw. It was even more complicated by the fact that Jerry was possessive. He would question her constantly about Jack, Brad and of course Nick and Kale. He didn't even like her talking to Layla or her sisters.

Layla met the brothers a year before when Sonja stayed with them for the week. Her car broke down pulling into the driveway because of the hole in front of the brother's home. Layla gave her a ride to work all week before the Jetta came from the dealership. Layla drooled over the boys all week long, only reminding Sonja how much the two girls were alike. Neither gossiped at the office, they worked and kept everyone else in line. Jack has said more than once he couldn't imagine the office without one of them, let alone both.

"Are you safe there?" Jack asked, knowing now that the office would run with only one of the girls, if only for one day.

"Very. I wouldn't be any safer in Fort Knox."

"And these boys are good boys?"

"Absolutely find men." Layla said smiling ear to

ear.

"Layla..." Sonja scolded before turning her attention back to the very worried Jack. "They would defend me with their own lives."

She had no doubt they would put their own lives on the line. And not just for her either. While they were each going through college and working together, Kale called in late one day. When he finally got there over an hour late, he told the story.

He was driving in and encountered an anxious woman with car trouble on the side of the interstate. He pulled over, offering her help. She seemed frightened to him. She said "Thank you," that she needed a tow truck and didn't have a cell phone. Kale gave her his mobile. She made two calls with it and gave it back. They sat on the side of the interstate, her two kids in the back seat of her car asleep. His trustworthy and funny nature got her to laugh, then explain to him the bruise on the arm. Her somewhat hot-tempered husband had gone after one of the kids in a rage. She stopped him, loaded up the kids in the car and took off, only to have the car stop forty minutes from her brother's house.

She had barely finished the story when her husband pulled up. Kale tried to explain to the guy that he had just stopped for the lady on the side of the road. The guy got a lucky hit on Kale, then went after the wife, who ran down the embankment. The tow truck driver pulled up as the guy hit Kale and called the police. By the time the police got there, they had to call an ambulance for the guy. Kales' fists were black and blue for almost three weeks from beating the guy, but the wife and the children were safe.

Sonja assumed, given how protective the brothers felt towards her, the result would be the same, if not worse, if someone attacked her. Especially if it was Nick beating on Jerry.

Satisfied with the answer, Jack told her to pick out any rug she wanted and headed off to his office. Layla didn't move a muscle.

"You are not going back this time?" Layla looked amazed.

"No, should I?"

"No. Just had to ask."

"I'm done. He has court in a few weeks. I will stay with the boys until I find something else or until they kick me out."

"We both know that won't happen. Put down the file and talk to me."

Sonja reluctantly looked up to meet Layla's eyes.

"What about the boys?"

"Same as always. It won't change until I change it. I have no plans on doing that anytime soon. Can we get to business please?"

"I have everything taken care of for the day. Didn't expect you in here. Why don't we go find a rug?"

"Want to go shopping with me at lunch?" Sonja smiled for the first time since she passed Nick in the hall.

"Shopping of course. With you, not so much." Layla could already see Sonja saying no to so many nice things, because they weren't on her list.

"Smart ass." They headed out the door to the back warehouse in search of a new rug.

Lunch ended up being greasy pizza from the food court in the mall. Then shopping: new bathrobe, new towels, and a new set of bedding. The one she had used was a hand-me-down from the grandparents. It was nice, but she wanted something more suited to herself. She picked out a few new candles as well, with a good mixture of scents. By the time they were done, her trunk was stuffed. Sonja seemed determined to make the new room look as much like home as it felt.

No one said anything when they arrived a little late back from lunch. Their co-workers were shocked because Sonja was never late for anything—and lunch made twice in one day. Sonja spent the rest of the day reorganizing her office and talking to her sisters on the phone. She explained she no longer lived with Jerry, and why. Each sister offered to let her come and stay. Each got the same "no" from her. She didn't want to be coddled and conspired against by her sisters. It was bad enough having the brothers do it to her.

She finished the day with Jack and Brad loading the huge carpet in the back seat of the car. It was one time she was thankful for a convertible. She loved it as well in the summer but in February, even in Mississippi, she would grin and bare it. Throughout the day, she couldn't help but feel bad about her behavior that morning. The brothers were just trying their best to keep her safe.

Nick pulled up as the men headed back inside following Sonja. Her eyes smiled at him as she went in the doors, telling him she wasn't as mad as she had been when she stormed out of the house. She was right in saying she was perfectly safe at work. It was the drive to and from that worried him. There were too many places where someone could cause her to have an accident and no one would know. She came bouncing out with Layla, whom he remembered meeting a few times before. Sonja looked so carefree. She didn't look around the way he wanted her to. She barely watched for cars. Nick however was watching everything, most of all watching her. It made him feel like a peeping Tom or some kind of pervert, partly because he was enjoying it so.

She approached his car, thinking he was as prompt as she was: four o'clock sharp. Before she could even say hello, he was already throwing questions at her. "Why is the top down on your car?"

"Cause I have a rug in the back seat."

"I was gonna get that. Guess you are more qualified."

"You were going to buy me a rug? So sweet. You ready to head home?"

"With you? Anytime, darlin'."

Sonja shot back the look of "I can't believe you said that." Layla laughed the rest of the way to her car.

She turned up the music and buttoned up her coat before pulling out of the parking lot across three lanes of traffic. All the way home Nick stayed only a few feet behind her, even when she took off, playing with cars in traffic. She knew, if the circumstances were different, he could take off and leave her in the dust.

At home, he grabbed one end of the rug while she fumbled with the other. More than once he knocked her down, just to watch as the fire came alive in her eyes. He was right. She was far more qualified to find a rug. It fit perfectly in the space. When she opened the trunk for the rest of her packages, he was dumbfounded. "I thought you were at work today?"

"I was."

"How much shopping did you do?" He grabbed several bags while she grabbed the smaller breakables.

"Just lunch hour plus a little. I wanted to get everything done. Took Layla with me. This way you didn't have to follow me around the mall all night."

"Thank you for sparing me the mall. Thank you for taking Layla with you too. I didn't mean to sound like you had to explain yourself. Just amazed at the rate that you or any woman can shop."

"I knew what I wanted, went after it and left. I don't like to wander around."

"Made a list, didn't you?"

Sonja was infamous for her lists. She was over organized and sooner or later those around her caught that bug. Except for Kale, nothing on this earth could make him organized or clean, not even Sonja.

"Yes I made a list."

She pouted a little. He made it sound like her tendencies were more anal than they really were. She directed him to set the bags on her bed.

"It's not a bad thing, darlin'. It's part of who you are."

Their eyes caught for a moment. He was actually admiring her for the way she was instead of trying to change her—the way Jerry did. If her heart hadn't pounded the night before when love floated through his eyes, now it did.

Sonja turned, mouth half open, to find him already out the door. She could hear his steps echo through the house and out the back door. Her heart told her to go after him to seize the moment but her body couldn't move. Her mind couldn't find the right words or actions. It would happen when she was ready, that much she was sure.

Busying herself, she unloaded all the bags and arranged the new candles in her bedroom and bathroom. The new towels lined the open shelves next to the bathtub. She chose a paler blue than the tiles on the floor, which was a nice complementary color and matched her bedroom nicely. The spa green in the bedding contrasted with the cherry finish on her new furniture, the rug a perfect match. The bed looked inviting—not that it hadn't before, but she hoped she would sleep better under the blanket.

Even though she spent the day cleaning her office, she wanted to dig down at her new home too. She pulled out every cleaning supply she found in the house, and started in Nick's bathroom.

The bathroom smelled of pine and disinfectant by the time she finished. The tiles sparkled like new, not that it was all that dirty to begin with. She then dusted everything and took a mop over his floor. She mopped down the hall, and then her room, bathroom and library. The entire house was beginning to smell like pine and flowers.

Sonja tackled Kale's room next, just a little after five. Even though he objected to it, she knew he would love it. She took all his laundry out, organized his entire room, and dusted it, thankful she didn't find a snake anywhere. The bathroom she scrubbed until, she was sure, if she cleaned any more, she would start scrubbing off the pattern on the tiles. The thought brought about a smile remember Grandma Badeaux's dishes. She was just finishing up the floor as Kale showed up in his doorway, dirtier than she ever remembered seeing him.

"What are you doing?" He grumbled from under the baseball cap.

"What does it look like I'm doing? Cleaning up after a pig."

"Oink! Oink! I told you this wasn't necessary. Hope you didn't go pokin' through my stuff."

"If you are talking about the dirty magazines in the bottom drawer of your nightstand. Interesting. Not as good as the real thing."

"Don't remind me." Her brashness couldn't

shock him. She took everything as if she had grown up with three brothers instead of sisters. Nothing ever embarrassed her—at least not that she would show. Deciding to play, he grabbed her causing her to drop the mop and squeal. "Who's the piggy now."

He dropped her on his fresh sheets, while she laughed the whole way, then pinned her to the bed. "Real thing is better, it has been long enough I don't remember. Want to refresh my memory?"

No matter what she tried, he wouldn't stop tickling her and she couldn't stop laughing. His facial stubble tickled her neck as he growled in her ear. If anything she was afraid he was getting everything she just cleaned dirty again.

He would be happy to take her, if it wouldn't kill his brother. Nevertheless, having a little innocent fun was never out of the question—except he was driving himself insane.

"Let me up, you filthy lunatic, you smell worse than your bathroom did."

"Never! Unless you promise you won't waste energy cleaning my room."

"Can't make that promise, and you know you love a clean room as long as you don't have to do it."

"True. So true. Now how about that romp."

Nick stood quietly in the hallway half amused, wondering if he should go push his brother off the bed and take up asking for a 'romp'. Her laughter warmed him from the inside out. He finally decided to break it up as nice as he could.

"Dinner is almost ready you two."

Sonja's eyes almost popped out of her head at the sound of Nick's voice. What must this look like to him?

Kale on the other hand was almost laughing,

trying not to make it apparent to his brother. "When I'm done here. Do I ever interrupt you when you're disrobing a beautiful girl?"

Sonja pushed this time with everything she had, landing him on his butt between the bed and the door. As he connected with the floor, he finally let out the laugh.

"I will be down as soon as I grab a shower. Start without me." Kale managed between laughs and headed toward the bathroom.

"I just cleaned in there."

"Yah, yah!" He shut the door before she could mother him anymore.

Picking up her cleaning supplies, she saw Nick eyeing her. She knew he wanted to be ornery like his brother but didn't want to push her boundaries. So she decided she would push his. She added a little bit of a sway to her hips trying her best Mae West impersonation.

"What you want a romp too, big boy?"

More than anything on this earth, he kept to himself. As well as, *Only if I can have the whole package, as long as it doesn't hurt Kale, and when you are ready.* "Not like that." Is what he finally settled on.

He didn't move out of the door way as she slid past him. Between Kale jumping on her, Nick catching them and then being so close to him, she was ready to romp with someone. Instead she assumed she would spend the rest of the night cleaning the downstairs. Working off sexual frustration, man frustration, and work frustration.

Sonja washed her hands then sat down to dinner with Nick, alone. Not that alone bothered her . . . other than the fact she was already bothered.

Bothered. Something else I get to add to

temperamental. That list just seems to keep growing.

"She cleaned my shower so well I almost slipped and broke my neck." Kale disturbed the silence before he hit the last step.

"Good payback for pinning me to your bed."

"No, payback for that would be staying pinned to my bed."

"No that would be pay forward. A little satisfaction for a little satisfaction. Payback is you pinning me to your bed unwillingly, then slipping in the shower, which I cleaned."

"Looked willing when I walked in." Nick added trying not to smile.

"I wasn't… I didn't…" The brothers laughed as she tried to fight back. "You two are just wrong. Treat me like that and I'll stop cleaning."

"Good!" Kale bit back.

"Not good. Your room needed it." Nick said

"See he's a little pig isn't he?" Sonja couldn't help but smile.

"In more ways than one." Nick was thinking about Kale on top of her again.

"I second that." Sonja finished off. They sat together as Kale finished his dinner.

Sonja jumped up grabbing dishes. Nick again tried to stop her. "Not tonight, you cooked, I'll do the dishes." Sonja said.

"I can do the dishes." Kale added.

"You had a dirty day at work and I've seen your room. I'm not sure I want to eat off anything you claimed to clean."

"Hey…" Kale started to object, "oh, never mind."

The brothers got up from the table and headed outside, leaving her to do something she loved:

cleaning. Each kissed her head as they walked by.

The dishes were clean and the patterns intact. Then she scrubbed down the kitchen thoroughly, while doing laundry, mostly Kale's. When she finished, it was going on eight and the boys were still outside taking care of their horses. She pulled a six-pack of beer out of the fridge and headed out to join them.

They enjoyed the rest of the night lounging outside, nursing beers.

"You don't have to follow me around tomorrow." Sonja jumped in as they were finishing the last of the beer before going in for the night.

"We don't have to, but we will." Kale responded without a thought, remembering the lengthy conversation on the phone between him and Nick first thing Friday morning. They had decided she wasn't moving and she wasn't going anywhere, that they could help, by herself.

"Jerry isn't in the hospital anymore and I'm not sure how mobile he is. We will take no chances." Nick piped in quickly.

"Jack gets to work every day before me I will call him to come out when I'm a block away. Nick should get home just before me every day if not shortly after. I promise everything will be fine." The brothers exchanged looks, then stared at her. "Quit conspiring against me. You're worse than my sisters. They have me moving back to Memphis and set up on dates with different guys each of them already knows. The last thing I need is to be treated like a child that can't take care of myself. I put him in the hospital and now I have a knife instead of a lamp."

"What if he hits you with a car when you are driving or walking?" Nick couldn't help but voice his concerns he had watching in the parking lot today.

While it was Kale's turn to have his eyes bug out of his head.

"Too many witnesses. Anything he does, he will want in private, just me and him." The thought worried them all a little more.

"Fine we won't follow you around, but if anything happens…" Nick started to agree.

"I have myself to blame." Didn't relieve him of the awful feelings.

"You will also call us if you come home early or leave work unexpectedly." Nick finished.

"Deal!"

As the beer emptied they each headed off to bed Nick slept deeply for the first time since she walked in the front door. His dreams were filled with her pinned to his bed.

9.

She woke Tuesday morning feeling good. The clock informed her it was only five in the morning but she was awake and wanting a shower. Her bathroom only contained the bathtub so she grabbed a towel, her soaps, and robe and snuck into Nick's room.

As she tiptoed through the door, she couldn't help but stop. No matter how many times she had seen him without a shirt, she still loved the look of his skin. Tight, tan, a slightly hairy chest. A light snore coming from him caused her to scurry across to the bathroom. The light showed her that it was still clean—as she assumed it would be. She chose his shower partly for that reason and partly because that she didn't want to be naked if Kale pinned her to his bed again for invading his room. Nick would just smile at her and say something cute like, 'Thanks for warming it up for me.' Then let her tactfully sneak back to her own room.

The shower was good, it was hot, and it was refreshing. Somewhere in her brain, she wanted him to not be such a gentlemen, to be a little more like his brother. At least touch her, another kiss, a little insight into his brain would be best. Something more than the love his eyes showed.

When she stepped out of the shower, she dried her body and wrapped her hair in the towel. Her hand just grabbing her robe as the bathroom door opened.

Nick stretched out, remembering the dreams that filled his night. They were getting better everyday. He was ready for a shower and to see her smiling face. He pushed open the bathroom door not remembering why he shut it. He saw more than her smile. He closed his eyes putting to memory everything he just saw. Her bare skin and her curves most of all. His dreams would improve even more from this point on. He stepped backwards with his hand still on the doorknob eyes shut tight trying his best not to reopen them.

"Too late to try and leave."

"Sorry didn't realize you were in here. What're you doin' in here?" He could hear the deepness in his voice hoping that she didn't.

"I don't have a shower, and your brother would have probably thrown me on his bed already." Not to say but she wished Nick would.

"Did you think to lock the door?"

"I did. I'm guessing its not working. I am fully covered, you can open your eyes."

Nick licked his lips still thinking about every inch of her. Then slowly opened his eyes to find her in a robe, a soft white robe he wanted to pull back off.

She stepped up to him, "Are you going to let me out? I know you're in shock from the sight of me naked but it couldn't have been that horrible."

"Wasn't horrible at all, darlin'." He watched her eyes, she was enjoying the compliment as much as the fact that she had left him speechless. "If you don't leave, I might have to behave like my brother."

"If you don't move I can't leave and no one is stopping you from behaving... badly." He stood there staring at her. He really wanted to act like his brother but knew she wasn't ready for anything serious and he couldn't take anything less. He leaned against the basin to let her by. She eased past him gently brushing against his body and out the door. Nick closed the door behind her and enjoyed a very cold shower.

When he came down stairs, she was already gone. His mind was moving. She wanted him to be a little bad. He would have been happy to oblige—when the time and circumstances were right.

Sonja finished another easy day at work, being in between projects drove her crazy. Too much time on her hands to think. She obsessed over Nick licking his lips, looking like he enjoyed the sight of her. She obsessed as well about the thought of him behaving like his brother, which was exactly what she wanted. Eventually she made phone calls, trying to get her next project. She thought about another shopping trip, but her promise to the boys about not going anywhere without them stopped that short. She was happy to be leaving at four o'clock sharp, accompanied to her car by Layla, with Jack looking out his office window and Brad standing near the front door. She found herself looking around the parking lot more than usual. Then she noticed his car parked halfway across the lot. He tried to hide it between two large SUVs but she would spot it anywhere. It was hard to miss a dark blue Mustang. Even harder to miss him behind the wheel. She watched as he dialed his phone, and hers rang.

"I was promised you wouldn't be following me around."

"I'm not following you. I'm watching you, proudly." Nick's voice sent a hum through her body.

"Proud? Like an overbearing father?"

"There goes the dad thing again. No, not like a dad like someone that loves you and what wants you to be safe. The same way Kale feels . . . and followed you most of the way here this morning."

"Loves me and wants me to be safe? I thought that's what a dad did. I wouldn't know but I think ordering me around falls in there. Like, I can't go out without parental supervision." She started her car and heard his start through the phone. "Loves me and can't stop looking when I stand in front of them while naked—that would be a lover. Can't look would be a brother." She didn't know where she was going with this but she was going to get a reaction from him. "Any of those sound like you?"

"A little of each."

"A little of each would be something near incest. Father, brother, lover, sounds like a definition of incest, baby."

They continued the conversation as they pulled out of the parking lot.

"Incest . . . then Kale would be guilty too."

"That might be one reason neither of you have."

"Jerry would be that reason."

"Since we all have been making a few promises lately, broken or not. Can we promise to quit saying that name?" They stopped at a red light. He was silent. She looked in her mirror to find him staring straight at her. "Nick?"

"Until he's gone I don't think we can. You're the one that brought up reasons why you never dated either of us."

"You brought up incest."

"I'm gonna pull in up here and grab beer since it seems to be a nightly ritual at this point."

"Sure, like I said last night I should be fine all the way home."

"I didn't say I was hanging up."

"Okay, while you're in there, grab me something chocolate."

"Chocolate?"

"Yes anything sweet and rich."

"You just described me."

It was the closest thing he ever said as a pickup line to her. Her heart pounded with the thought. She watched him turn into the little store as she slowed down stopping at another light. Listening to the sounds coming from around him, she knew she was silent for too long.

"If I was describing you I could use those words as well as 'conservative,' 'nutty,' and 'loveable,'" she said.

"You think I'm loveable?"

She heard the door to a refrigerator open then close.

"You are feeling frisky today aren't you? Out of all the words I just said that's the one you pick out."

"Frisky! I saw you naked this morning."

She laughed until she heard him say thanks to the cashier. "You just said that in front of a total stranger?"

"He has no idea who I'm talking to. I figured after me walking in on you and Kale yesterday you didn't mind being public."

"That was different… Dang it!"

"You don't have to yell at me."

"I'm not, there is a car wreck on the bridge."

"Stuck, huh?"

"Yeah I am. You might want to go around the other way." She looked around her checking out the other cars making sure Jerry wasn't near.

"You sure you're okay."

"I didn't say I was hanging up."

Nick took the other way to the house. It was normally only a fifteen-minute drive the way she went and twenty the way he went. Car wrecks on the bridge could cause a two-minute to a two-hour back up.

"How about a movie tonight?" He asked.

"What do you have in mind?"

"How about a little romance?" He wanted to flirt. He felt as if his brother had taken over his body.

"Right now that doesn't sound much like a movie." *Sounds like this conversation*, she thought. "How about comedy, we could all use a good laugh this week."

"Action?"

"Nightmares."

"Scary?"

"Why? So I have to chose which of you to cuddle up to in those parts that I can't stand to watch."

Not that she wouldn't do it on purpose. Burying her head in Nick's bare shoulder would make her night great.

"Good point."

She heard him shut off the car and close the door. Video store.

"Do we have popcorn at the house?"

"Should."

He kept in mind three movies, one was a sequel to something they all saw at the movies a while back, one night when Jerry was "working late." Then one of whatever she suggested. He might have to pick up something scary just for the fun of it. "Finally through! Car hit the rail, didn't go over. You gonna worry about me gettin' to the house before you?"

"Not for the maybe five minutes tops that you will be there—and you still aren't hangin' up."

"I like the phone option more than you actually

following me."

"I like the following you that way I know that you are fine."

"After this morning you should know I'm fine."

He laughed loud enough that everyone in the video store looked at him. He could feel his face going red. "That was so wrong and I never said your body wasn't."

"Payback for what you said in front of the cashier at the store. You like my body?"

"I will get you for that and there isn't a man alive that wouldn't like that body."

"Promise?"

"No. Threat."

He could hear her laughing as he paid for the movies and headed out to his car. Her laugh became choppy. The line was breaking up. He forgot about the two-mile stretch with no cell phone service.

"Sonja.... Sonja...." He looked at the screen finding the call gone. He pulled out of the video store, foot to the floor.

Sonja saw the black BMW parked down the road from the mailbox. She in turn stopped in front of the neighbor's drive. She knew that car. Glancing at her phone, she realized it was back in service. Her call went to Nick's voice mail, which told her he was already in the dead zone. Pushing the button to lock the doors, she looked around without moving her head. Nothing changed for almost two minutes. Then the car down the road started moving.

She didn't think about it. She popped her car into reverse and pushed the pedal as far as it would go. The road, from its beginning to the mailbox, was a little over half a mile and she parked almost in the middle of that. She kept her eyes on the end of the road only a quarter of a mile away, glancing forward to see if he was moving faster than she. The quarter mile she started with was almost half gone when she saw Nick turn the corner behind her. The opening in the field for work trucks to enter was just big enough for her to whip into hopefully without have to slow down. She did it without touching her brakes. He flew past her.

She heard brakes grinding, too scared to open her eyes. Her cell phone made her jump and let out a little scream.

"Stay in your car." She heard his car door open, the noises around him going soft as he dropped the phone in a pocket.

"I thought I told you to stay away." Nick shouted across to where Jerry stopped his car as soon as he saw Nick's.

"I want the key to my apartment."

"I'll drop it in the mail."

"I want to talk to her."

"I will put you back in that hospital."

"You know I can have you arrested for threatening me. I will talk to her sooner or later."

"Little worm. Try it. Its not a threat." Nick wanted to pull him out of the car, knowing Jerry would try to run him over if given the chance. If Jerry succeeded that would leave Sonja with only the knife to defend herself.

"You're blocking a public road." Each word from Jerry sounded a little more egotistical than the previous.

She heard a car door open and close. Breathing a little easier as she saw Nick's car back up to the front of hers. Jerry passed by slowly, looking straight at her, anger in his eyes that she had seen twice before in her lifetime. She didn't look away until he was out of sight. She wouldn't give him the satisfaction of knowing she was scared. And then she cried.

The knock on her window made her jump. Nick standing on the other side pleading with her to open the door. Through tear filled eyes, she fumbled for the door handle.

When the door finally gave, Nick yanked it open, pulling her out. His lips against her face didn't stop the tears as he wrapped his arms around her. "It's okay, Sonja. He won't hurt you. I'll see to it."

He smoothed her hair, gently rocking her side to side, as she left tear stains on his shirt. Her body tightened even more as a honk from the road disrupted their silence. "What are you two doing down here?"

Nick glared across to Kale who stood out the driver's side of his truck. "Jerry . . ."

The one word response from Nick said it all. The anger in that word actually helped Sonja quit crying. As her arms loosened, he let his slip down her sides. When he finally caught her eyes again he asked, "Better?"

"Much. Thank you, again." There was so much more she wanted to say. So much his eyes were saying to her. *All in due time*, she said to herself to settle the inner conflict.

"Lets go home and watch a movie," Nick said still caressing her hair.

Her heart said to hold him, don't let him get in the car and go. The way he was standing with his legs apart made him just a little taller than she was. Taking advantage of his height, she kissed his forehead. Slowly, gently, as if the skin were his lips.

When her feet found the ground, she opened her eyes again, nodding her head as she agreed. "Home."

His eyes were questioning if this was the right time, if he should whisper the words in her ear. His arms betrayed him, letting her slip out and into her car. Nick shut the door, slowly making his way back to his car. Only halfway back he stopped, turning to find her sad eyes watching him.

They chose to watch the sequel after they ate dinner. Sitting in the middle of the leather couch, she was enjoying the movie. Popcorn in her lap and chocolate covered peanuts in hand. The cares of the day behind her, she wrapped her brain around the movie. Nick sitting so close she could cuddle up to him, she could lean over and kiss him. She wasn't ready for that.

Nick sat where he could see the driveway and road. Kale watched his brother's face, waiting for a sign that he needed to get outside.

Each time Nick looked to Sonja she seemed engrossed in the movie, her eyes wild with the thoughts the pictures on the screen were invoking. One word came to his mind: gorgeous. And he wouldn't let Jerry change the way she was. Not anymore.

He took his seat in the library that night, anger fueling him instead of sleep.

10.

Wednesday morning they danced again in Nick's bathroom, this time the robe was on when he knocked on the door. Kale seemed to always have breakfast ready and Nick did the dishes quickly before he left for work. The breakfast conversation didn't last long. Sonja didn't fight on any point, hardly said anything more than 'I agree'. She parked her car in the back behind the pine trees that separated yard from pasture and rode to work with Kale. Somewhere in her heart, she knew that anything the brothers suggested was for the best. She dropped the key in the mail before lunch. No return address, no letter. Only a key and Jerry's address. After lunch, she called Detective Ivan.

When Sonja finished the brief explanation of the night before, the detective tried his best to explain the law. He informed her that Jerry could file a formal complaint on any threats from Nick or Kale, but if neither ever touched him then there wouldn't be any issues. He checked on his computer and found no such complaints. Without a formal complaint it would be the brothers word against Jerry. Considering their records, Jerry would lose the battle before it started. He quickly added he would keep an eye out for anything on the computer with the name "Badeaux" on it.

After five times of spelling "Badeaux," the detective had it right. Since Jerry had a valid reason for stopping by—his key, there was nothing the law could do. If he became a nuisance, started to follow her, or called the office then they could get a restraining order. Thanking the detective again for his help, she hung up. She was worried sick that Nick at some point would end up in jail for protecting her from Jerry. Or worse, he might land in the hospital.

Nick picked her up at four sharp, singing all the way home. When Nick used his clutch to make the car jump, she laughed. Both of them kept an eye out for Jerry.

The rest of the week crept by on pins and needles. Everyone was wound a little too tight. Each day was better than the one before because it was another day without a visit from Jerry.

Choosing to spend most of their time in the backyard, the brothers taught Sonja more about swords and bows, ways of defending herself in general. Kale constructed a foam dagger so she could practice stabbing Nick. He took her to the ground when she made a move to stab him below the belt. Proud again that she thought about using that to her advantage, he got up from that attack breathless from rolling around on the ground with her—though not because she put up a fight.

She showed them that she could move quicker than they could when she did a back flip to get away from Kale. It was after she almost shot him with an arrow accidentally. Then she showed them other acrobats that she could still do. Nick almost drooled and Kale was in pain when she did the splits. She enjoyed them watching her. Maybe she was a little bit voyeuristic herself when it came to the brothers.

Friday night while eating dinner, they explained the Renaissance festivals they attended, or at least tried to explain.

"We fight." Kale looked at her as if she was

dim, he got the same look back.

They had invited her more than once to come to a festival with them. She declined each of them to spend time with Jerry on the weekends. She ended up spending most of the time alone anyway. "You and a few other guys spend a day banging on each other using swords, horses, and whatever else you can get your hands on?"

"More or less." Kale nodded.

"Why?"

"Fun and the kiss of a pretty girl at the end." Kale smiled.

"Now you're confusing me more."

"Let me try." Nick came out of the kitchen and showed a case of beer to them. They left the dirty dishes and headed to the backyard. When they were settled on the picnic table, he started. "We fight, like we've been teaching you to. To start off with, we use the horses to joust, which means we take really long poles and try to knock each other off our horses."

"Why?"

Nick laughed at her, which was a beautiful sound in her ears.

"We are recreating the way they fought for sport and pride in the Renaissance era."

"Why?"

This time he didn't laugh, she was truly concerned and bewildered.

"For sport and pride, the fun and the adrenaline."

This time she laughed. "Do you all ever actually get hurt?"

They both looked away, neither wanting to jump in this time.

"Take that as a yes."

"Normally only a few bruises and maybe a cut or two." Nick wasn't going to add his concussion when he took a brutal fall from his horse. Or the fact that Kale had more than once broken a rib, let alone that Nick had been the one to break it, more than once.

"No gushing of blood? No massively broken bones?"

They both shook their heads,

"What about minor injuries?"

They looked away again.

"And ya'll actually want me to go next weekend and watch?"

"You're not good enough yet to enter. And we don't want to leave you at home since the jerk knows where you are staying." Kale was actually serious.

"Alright! Is it okay if I bring along Layla and bury my head when you are beating on each other, or someone else is beating on you?"

"You will love it so much you won't bury your head and Layla might like it too."

Nick was so relieved she agreed that he would have allowed anyone to come with her. And if Jerry showed up he would have enough swords at hand to make the worm look like Swiss cheese.

With that settled, they continued to tell her about the previous festivals, drinking beer in the backyard, under the oaks and stars.

The following week Kale took her to work, Nick took her home. She was getting accustomed to having chauffeurs. She didn't even mind when Layla took her to the doctors, where she was overjoyed to get a perfectly clean bill of health.

Monday they did the shopping, all three of them together. Since the boys had their competition over the weekend Sonja volunteered to cook dinner every night. She was happy to keep her hands busy while the boys practiced in the backyard.

Each time she heard one of them yell "ouch" her heart fell a little. Then it would lift when they started laughing a few seconds later. When one needed a break she even filled in. Perhaps practicing with her wasn't as good, but it was better than nothing—and each time she substituted she got better. They both thought she was doing well, especially when she smacked Nick on the shoulder on Thursday.

"Nick!" She heard her voice crack as a shot of pain flashed over his face.

"I can't believe you hit me."

"That makes three of us." Kale said as his brother took off his shirt to make sure it wasn't bleeding.

Sonja looked queasy as he removed his shirt. Not that seeing his bare skin caused it, though. That actually made her heart pump harder. The thought of hurting anyone with a sword was enough to make her ill. The fact that it was Nick made it worse.

"Lucky for you she didn't make you bleed."

"Lucky for her, too."

"You are the one that trusts me with a sword." She snapped back.

Nick took a shot toward her. She deflected it. "You're getting good darlin'."

"Darling?" She took an ornerier shot at him. He deflected it.

"No… Darlin'. What are you gonna do about it?"

She took another shot and he took away her sword. She chose to run and hide behind Kale, smiling shyly over his shoulder to Nick. Not since the dropped phone call and Jerry's appearance had they had fun in flirting. There had been a little flirting but no fun. From behind Kale, she batted her eyes while scanning over Nick's body, a fine body that would never do her harm, unless she asked for it. A fine body housing a wonderful person, a true friend. A body whose embrace she could lose herself in.

Glancing over his shoulder Kale could see how much fun Sonja was having. "Sir, you dare to brandish a weapon at this beautiful maiden?"

"Is the maiden yours to protect?" Nick asked back.

Sonja did her best to hold her head up and look astonished, like a spoiled princess.

"Yes!"

He took a shot at his brother as Sonja ran for the picnic table, jumping on top of it and quietly cheering on Kale as her protector.

"What if the maiden would rather come with me?" Nick asked, swinging at Kale.

"You assume much good sir." Sonja jumped in with a smile on her face, and more attitude than any women of yore could have shown, with her hands on her hips. "What gives you a thought like that?"

He stared at her, ornery as ever, while still keeping his brother at bay.

"Me thinks the lady has an eye for me, for some time now."

Kale took a cheap shot at Nick causing him to have to take his eyes off Sonja and meet his brother's stare. The look told him he was treading thinly.

"Again you presume much." Sonja said

"We will see."

He lowered his sword to his brother showing he conceded the fight for the night.

Kale jumped on the table and hugged Sonja, laughing as Nick walked in the house.

Nick glanced back to see Sonja watching him.

As Friday night came, the brothers grew more rambunctious and it was contagious. The three together loaded everything in the back of Kale's SUV, attached the horse trailer, and prepared to leave at six the next morning.

Sonja jumped out of bed at four thirty, too excited to go back to sleep. She enjoyed a hot bath, dressed, and started breakfast before anyone else stirred.

Standing over the kitchen stove listening to the bacon fry, Sonja thought of the day ahead. Watching the brothers do something they loved. The thought of them getting hurt brought her down a little, though nothing could ruin today in her mind.

The explosion of what sounded like glass coming from outside broke the early morning silence, tearing her out of her utopia. She jumped—a slight scream coming from her as the noise echoed through the house. From above her, she heard two sets of feet hit the floor with a dull thud. Then a little scampering and the brothers were coming down the stairs as tires peeled out from the road. Each hit the front door running, Nick with a sword in hand, Kale with a bow. No shoes, no shirts, just weapons. Sonja put her back against the island afraid if she didn't she would pass out. She held the tears, choosing to pray instead.

They saw the taillights almost at the end of the road when they got to the mailbox. Neither could make out the car from there through the morning fog, let alone the driver. They were certain, though, it was Jerry. When they realized that neither heard nor saw

Sonja when they ran out of the house, they ran back with as much force and speed. Nick was yelling her name as they saw the back of his car. The window busted out.

Kale's heart skipped a beat. He realized Nick didn't care about the car. He was worried for Sonja.

She was hard to miss, crying on the floor of the kitchen in the fetal position. Nick was the first to her. His knees sliding across the floor as he expressed his main concern. "Are you hurt?"

Nick's voice being so close and filled with worry, she jumped. Her eyes fell on his while he looked her over. Satisfying himself that she wasn't hurt, he pulled her into his arms, listening to Kale on the phone with the police.

Kale reached behind them and shut off the stove. He knew Nick wasn't going to move.

It took less than ten minutes for the police to get there and only fifteen for Detective Ivan to show. Nick held her in his arms until he sat her in one of the rocking chairs as they pulled a brick out of the back seat of the Mustang. It had crude writing on it that read, "She's mine."

"It will take a few days to get the brick back from the lab with fingerprinting and anything else they can give me." Detective Ivan explained as he eyed Nick and Kale on the front porch. He tried to size them up and make sure he wouldn't have to save Sonja from them as well. She looked so sad sitting in the rocking chair with a brother on each side. "Until we get the evidence we can't arrest him."

"But we know it was him."

Nick stayed so calm. Sonja's heart sank even further.

"An ID from half a mile away won't stick. Any

lawyer, even a bad one, would be able to pick it apart."

Sonja couldn't deny liking the detective. He told it to her straight, unwilling to sugar coat anything.

"Is there anything we can possibly do, Detective?" Kale was for once. Everyone seemed to appreciate it, even though Sonja really wanted him to make her laugh.

"Well the best I can do is to keep a car in the area just in case. I'd say best you can do is keep her safe."

Sonja was impressed as they took measurements of the tire tracks. She was sure that wasn't routine. The detective was after Jerry with a vengeance.

"Detective Ivan, thank you again. Can't seem to say that enough lately. May I pry and inquire why you want him so badly?"

The detective met each of their worried faces. "My dad beat my mom to death when I was twelve. It's why I became a cop and why I'm called in anytime there is a domestic violence report. It's an obsession for me."

"An obsession I'm very lucky you have. Can I get that restraining order now?"

"If anything can be linked to Jerry then yes. You all going on a trip?" He gestured to Kale's truck that was thankfully untouched.

"Down to the fairgrounds for the Renaissance festival," Nick stated with his hand resting on Sonja's shoulder. He hadn't taken his hands off her since they were on the kitchen floor.

"You all play in the games they have down there?" Detective Ivan asked.

"Yes sir, every time."

"I might have to stop in and check it out."

"Anytime. We practice right in the backyard if

you don't make it out today."

"Thanks, son. We should be out of your hair in a few more minutes."

"You hungry, Sonja?" Nick bent down to her level.

"Not really but there is a huge breakfast in there for you. Both of you will need the energy. I'm sorry its cold by now."

Nick kissed her cheek. "You come inside when they leave. Me and Kale will yell when we are ready."

Sonja nodded. They left her on the front porch watching the detective and police do what they do best.

"They are pretty good boys aren't they?" The detective asked as they went inside.

"I couldn't have better friends, Detective."

"Good to know. I'll let you get inside."

Once again, she could only nod.

It was starting and she felt helpless. Jerry could have just as easily sent the brick through a window in the house. Then come through the window, taking her away. He could have also stood in the front yard and shot each brother as they came out the door. He could have set the beautiful house on fire, everyone asleep inside would be trapped and die. The possibilities were endless and ran through her head at light speed. Somehow, she kept the tears from falling.

While he and Kale quickly ate, Nick was wrestling with the same concerns as Sonja. She looked half comatose from this morning events and there was nothing he could do or say to change it.

Less than five minutes later, the detective had everyone pulling out. He collected shoeprints, tire tracks, and the brick. If any of it matched Jerry, he was hauling him in. He gave a healthy nod to Sonja as he got in his car to leave.

Within ten minutes, the boys were loading up the horses. She wandered back inside and threw some breakfast into a Ziploc hoping she would get hungry at some point. She cleaned up the kitchen until they yelled at her to come on. She double-checked each lock and headed out the door, hoping they would have a home to come back to. Smiling the best she could as she rounded the corner of the house, she jumped in Kale's truck for a day at the fair.

11.

They pulled into the fairgrounds just before seven as the sun shone through the pines. Watching all the people hustle and bustle about, she began understanding a little about why they liked the sport; the air was brimming with excitement. Sonja helped as much as she could in unloading the horses and getting their gear set up. Other competitors occupied an individual tent, but the brothers chose to share one. They knew everyone and introduced her as a friend and new roommate to each. She quickly learned that the competitors preferred to be called "knights," a term she found fitting for her two. There were fifteen in all competing this round, and then Marcus who ran the show.

She remembered Marcus as the friend from whom she purchased her beautiful bedroom set. He asked about it and, smiling she told him how much she loved it. Some of the other men had wives and children. Most loved to watch the show. The ones who couldn't take it went shopping in the fair or the closest mall.

Layla arrived as they were finishing the unpacking around eight. The fair was just opening. The boys reluctantly let Sonja walk around with Layla before the competing started at nine. Though they didn't tell her, they took turns watching her as she went.

The fairgrounds were dusty but no one seemed to mind, her least of all. The entire event was beginning to seep into her blood. The booths were set up in small wooden buildings or tents like those in which the knights were preparing. She enjoyed shopping and talking with Layla. Sonja updated her on the events of the morning while she was on her cell phone making an appointment with the dealership to replace Nick's window.

They went through each booth. She found many things she loved and a few she wanted to buy for the boys. One advantage to living with Jerry was that she saved up a lot of money. She never went anywhere or did anything, didn't spend money except on the occasional movie and what she bought for nieces and nephews. Jack paid her well. Plus, each time an account was complete, she got a bonus. The Roland bonus was enough to replace Nick's entire car if she needed to and still have enough to buy whatever she wanted. She never told Jerry that she made bonuses.

The weapon smith drew her attention most of all. A sign hanging over the wooden building said "William's Steel." He had everything he needed to make swords right on the spot, a hot fire, fresh water, an anvil and more hammers than Sonja ever saw in her life. His wife, Agnes, waited on customers while he crafted his art. She cussed at him when he sent hot sparks flying her way. Then she apologized to everyone else, saying William was a buffoon—talented but still a buffoon. Sonja had two swords set back for the boys, wanting their approval before she took them. Not approval for buying sword, but for the specific choices she had made. She put one in her bag for herself and paid for them all. She picked out an elegant peasant gown and some jewelry before nine came around.

Nick felt odd again following her around when he relieved his brother of the duty. He watched everything she admired, even approved of the swords she picked out. He blushed thinking about her in the peasant gown and hoping he could take it off her at some point. He heard the girls talking about the pewter candlesticks. Sonja said she had enough candlestick holders, even though they were so unique, she didn't need more. Nick snuck in and bought them, still able to keep an eye on her.

The small stadium consisted of the stands, ten rows of benches curved around one side of an open field. There was a railing across so no one would fall the five feet onto the field. The families of the other knights saved a seat for her in the front row where she wouldn't miss a thing—and had no one to hide her face behind.

Marcus opened the celebration with two men, one on either side of him, blasting trumpets. They looked like court jesters. He on the other hand had rode on a beautiful horse in what looked like royal garments of purple and black. His booming voice echoed as he spoke, with a very nice British accent that he didn't have the previous two times she had spoken with him.

"Lords and Ladies welcome to the our festival today and thank you for coming. You are about to see fifteen of our best fighters come together for honor and glory to winning today's challenges." The knights came out from both sides of the arena to line up behind him as the crowd cheered. Even though they were wearing full armor, Sonja could still point out Nick and Kale to Layla.

"Each gentlemen has on a color, so you can cheer for your favorite, or *favorites* to win." Marcus glanced at Sonja as he accentuated 'favorites'. She didn't really care who won as long as neither brother got hurt. *Oh, Lord please don't let them get hurt.*

"Each rider will give a banner to a special lady in the audience so he will fight especially for her in hopes of winning her affection and perhaps a small kiss if he is victorious."

A kiss, her mind swam trying to not drown. *How could I forget the kiss?*

They watched as each rider chose someone in the audience to receive his banner and flower. Sonja watched Kale prance his stud toward them. She was worried about taking a banner from either brother, most of all Kale. Most days he understood that Nick was the one who held her heart, always had and now—every day they were together—grasped it all the more tightly. Kale had some kind of hold on her, mostly like a brother. She assumed he had a valid reason for trying to stay in the middle between Nick and her. She only wished he would share those reasons. When he arrived at the railing, he opened his helmet, "Lady Layla."

Layla's mouth almost dropped open as Sonja tried not to look at her, tried not to snicker.

Sonja was smiling at Kale, who winked back, thankful for Sonja's approval.

Layla took his flag and bowed graciously. As she sat back down she whispered, "I can not believe he did that."

"I'd say it's a good thing."

Sonja kept an eye on Nick who was slowly going toward the middle of the crowd. She watched as husbands gave their wives banners and they in turn kissed the helmets. Those that didn't have family in the audience chose young girls, while Nick slowly made his way to her. He left down his helmet and motioned her to come nearer. The thought of saying no thrilled her. The thought of a kiss at the end pushed her. Handing her drink to Layla, she stood up and walked to the railing, never taking her eyes off him. "Dost the lady have an eye for me?"

"Good sir, you presume much." She was amazed at herself when she said it with a straight face.

"Perhaps I should choose another to give this token to."

She couldn't hide the smile anymore. He knew as well as she did, he wouldn't.

"If my knight must ask the question, then my knight doesn't know me well."

Nick held out the banner. Then pulled it away as she reached for it.

"I expect a kiss at the end of my ride."

"If you win I will consider that option." *Consider his lips touching hers. Consider how much she loved him.*

He held it again, saving her from talking to herself to long. She took it slowly then watched him ride away to rejoin the rest of the knights. Sitting down she opened the banner to find an orchid in the center. She slid it in her hair. Having found her knight and her flower, she yearned to discover where her heart had gone.

Sonja couldn't see his face but he was smiling ear to ear. He won the last two championships, and had no plans on losing this one. Those lips against his at end of the day. He wanted them against his lips and not his forehead. Wanted her to give them freely.

The crowd watched as each pairing took to the field. Sonja soon learned that the brothers had kept a lot of information away from her. She watched as the poles, that Marcus told the crowd were lances, shattered when they hit a rider. She turned her head as bodies hit the ground when knocked off the horse. When Nick was up she cheered, then hid her face in her hands, almost running to the field when she thought he took too long to get up. Layla grabbed her so she couldn't. Her body flinched as the knights exchanged blows with their swords. She could see by the third match Nick's shoulder where she left a bruise was bothering him at least a little, no one else in the crowd seemed to have noticed.

Nick was having fun as always, but he wanted to hold and comfort her when she hid her face. He wanted to whisper to her when she flinched. The other men got a few shots in on him because he was worried about her.

She figured quickly that it was a process of elimination, each brother won their first match, and moved to the second, they won those and moved to third. Each time there was a match, someone didn't return to the field. They alternated the odd man out into the line up until they had an even number and then went on. By the third round, they were down to four men total. Nick drew a barbarian of a man, he stood almost 6' 5" and at least three hundred pounds, mostly muscle. Kale drew the other guy who was almost his equal in size and very quick.

She sat on the edge of her seat, almost sick watching Kale and the guy chop away at each other. Kale gave as good as he got. It seemed like forever, Layla informed her it was less than five minutes and Kale had the guy on the ground, his sword halfway across the arena. As Nick pranced into the arena, Marcus informed everyone that Kale would be going to the final round.

The worry etched across her face pulled at Nick's heart as he saw her reach for her cell phone. He assumed it was ringing since he couldn't hear it between the helmet and cheering crowd. He watched her plug one ear with her finger as she talked to whoever was on the other end. He got the signal from Marcus and took off across the field.

Sonja could barely hear the Detective.

"Miss Mitchell I'm sorry to interrupt your festivities. I'm guessing your boys are doing well?"

"So far very well. Thank you, Detective." She turned to watch as Nick took off across the field. She flinched again as the lances struck, neither knight falling off their horse.

"I called because nothing matched Jerry."

". . . What?" Her confusion echoed in the detective's ear.

"I said—"

"No. . . How can that be?" She watched as each rider took off again with a new lance in hand.

"We're guessing he hired someone that couldn't be traced back to him."

They hit each other, Nick flew off the side of his horse, her heart dropped, tears welling up in her eyes as she took her seat again. Not sure if she wanted the phone call to go on. Knowing she wanted him off the field.

"What's next?" She asked.

"I'd say you should stay close to those two boys of yours."

She saw Kale standing below her.

Kale had one eye on his brother as he crawled to his feet, one eye on Sonja as she took the call. He could see she wasn't doing well. What was causing the pain wasn't so clear.

"I'd say Mr. Lane is pretty much afraid of them." The detective continued.

"As he should be."

Nick drew his sword as he stood.

"If we find the guy we will get him and Jerry, but I can't say it looks good."

"Thank you, Detective, for your honesty again." Nick took a shot to the ribs of his armor. He was wielding the sword with his right arm, the arm she hadn't hit him on.

"I'd also be on the look out for a man standing around 6' 2" say two hundred and twenty pounds. That's as close as I know from the tracks in the yard."

Sonja watched as Nick gave two good hits to the barbarian.

"Is that the guy that threw the brick?"

"Yeah. Don't have finger printing back yet. I'm gonna get to work here, I'll give you another ring if anything new happens."

"Thank you." She hung up the phone as Nick gave two, and received one. Kale looked at her questioningly as she flinched. She crawled down to be as close as she could as she relayed what the detective told her.

"Nick's not gonna like that." Kale said as she finished.

"I'm not liking this."

She flinched again, as he took a good hit in the right shoulder. He switched hands again. It was over in three hits, when he took the barbarians sword out of his hands.

Nick could see Sonja and Kale, their faces telling him the phone call wasn't good. When John hit his shoulder, it sent shooting pains through his body, pushing him harder. He flipped the sword to the other hand and took after him. He had no choice but to sit and breathe after he took the sword.ABondering if his brother would take the win if he conceded.

"Thank god that is over." She couldn't help but

breathe easier.

"My turn to beat on my brother."

"Kale!"

He pretended he didn't hear her as he walked out of the arena.

"Five minutes Lords and Ladies. While the last two prepare for battle." Marcus boomed over the crowd.

Nick got on his horse, with a little help from the barbarian. His eyes didn't leave her as she stood at the railing. She would not motion to make him stop, but her body language was hopeful he would. He rode out of the arena meeting Kale in their tent. Kale applied some more ointment to his brother's shoulder as he passed along the information from Sonja.

Sonja watched as the defeated men walked into the arena taking the center of the field in front of the stands to watch the final match up.

"One of us is about to get a kiss." Layla leaned over.

"Layla as long as they both leave today in one piece they will each get a kiss, from both of us as far as I'm concerned."

"You would let me kiss Nick?"

"If it gets this over with. If they would come back less black and blue. And not on the lips. Yes!"

They couldn't help but laugh.

Less than three minutes and Nick rode into the stadium stopping in front of the barbarian that he just defeated. Kale came in the other side. The barbarian nodded his head as Nick spoke to him. Nick then rode to his side of the field taking the lance from a young kid, whom Marcus called a squire.

The barbarian walked around into the stands

taking a seat next to Sonja.

"Hello Miss Sonja. My name is John." The big man spoke slowly, and soft enough that only she could hear. "Nick would feel better if you had someone sitting next to you for this."

"Thank you but I don't think you can help my heart from pounding out of my chest."

"No, but I can take down a guy that's six two, and two twenty. Unless it's Nick."

"Nick's not that big." She said, not taking her eyes off him as he fixed the grip on the lance.

"No, but he's Nick."

She nodded her head that she understood, turning her eyes back to the field as each brother took off.

When they got to the point where the lances would collide, she closed her eyes. After a few heart wrenching seconds of not hearing the unmistakable noise, she opened them again to find them sliding off the horses, swords in hand. John let out a boisterous laugh as Sonja buried her head in her hands.

"Are you two ever going to joust?" Marcus' voice boomed across the arena.

Each brother took off his helmet as Nick yelled back at Marcus. "This is much more fun."

"For our newcomers while the brothers remove their armor. Anytime it is the two of them, this is what they do. They forget the joust and go after the swords. They strip down to the basic chain and have at it. This is also where I must add don't try this at home."

Sonja couldn't keep her tongue any longer. "Why not? They do it."

"Oh dear lady," Marcus shook his head at her as she smiled back. "Living with them must be interesting."

"You don't know the half of it." The brothers began doing the dance she'd seen many times in the backyard.

Marcus yelled across a little confused. "Nicholas put that sword in the other hand. No fair giving your little brother an advantage."

"My shoulder hurts and he still can't beat me."

Kale took a shot at his brother, just catching the bad shoulder. Nick let out a hollow grunt as he went after him.

Kale added. "His shoulder hurts cause he let his guard down around a female."

Marcus looked at Sonja with eyebrows raised.

She could feel the embarrassment heating her face as she spoke, "He gave me the sword."

The crowd erupted in laughter, as the brothers where slowly pushing themselves toward the stands. Sonja was smiling watching them, not worrying for the first time that either would get hurt. She half hoped that Kale would win, receiving a kiss from Layla. In her mind, it was a perfect match.

"Miss Sonja." The barbarian whispered to her.

"Yes?"

"Do you know the guy down a bit in the tan shirt?"

Sonja glanced down the isle spotting the guy with a tan shirt, blue jeans, and tan work boots. He was watching her. While smiling at the brothers on the field, she leaned over to the barbarian. "No, John I don't."

Pulling her cell phone out of her purse, she dialed Detective Ivan, keeping her eyes on the brothers.

"Detective. You said you knew so much about the guy that threw the brick."

"Yes, Ms. Mitchell. Are you okay?"

"Classic tan work boots by any chance?"

"We can't be certain on the color, otherwise I'd yes."

"Would you like to come to the fair, cause I have this odd feeling that I found the guy?"

"Describe him."

"Like you said, six two, two twenty, blonde crew cut, square face. Military look to me."

"Not sure about it all but it looks like I'm coming to the fair, to check it out."

The line went dead, she wasn't smiling anymore, as her eyes met Nick's.

Nick already found the guy in the audience and the brothers were making their way back to the stands, smacking on each other, the audience loving the show.

After less than five minutes of the man in tan watching her, she saw Detective Ivan on the other side of the arena heading her way with two officers in tow.

Sonja watched as the man in tan stood and started walking towards her and away from the detective. Nodding to each other the brothers ran the rest of the way to the stands then jumped up on the railing. Their swords landing on either side of the guys throat before he took two steps from where he started from.

"Would you like to come with us?" Nick said between clenched teeth, caused by anger and the fact that his hurt shoulder was holding him on the rail.

The man in tan stared the brothers down. No one flinched. "I have no idea what you are talking about."

"It's alright boys, I got him. Sir, go with the officers *quietly*." The man in tan turned toward where Sonja sat—and his only possible exit. John stood up blocking his way. The man in tan put up his hands, the officers cuffed him and led him out of the stands. With a nod from the detective, the brothers jumped down from their perch and moved back to the center of the field. Nick dropped the sword into his left hand and the fight resumed.

After several minutes Marcus yelled across, "Would you two like to call this one a draw?"

The brothers, out of breath, stopped hitting each other. They were mostly worried about Sonja.

"We can call a draw?" Kale looked confused for a moment weighing the options.

"Either that or I concede to you, if you want a win that way. My shoulder hurts and I don't want to be this far away anymore."

Kale understood his brother was talking about Sonja.

"You would give up a kiss from Sonja?"

"She'll give me one sooner or later."

"You know she loves you."

"She loves you too." Nick said quickly.

"It's not the same."

Nick was amazed that they were having this talk here, now.

Kale continued, "I've run interference long enough. If she's not ready, the two of you will figure out when she is."

"Tie?" Nick asked.

"Agreed."

Sonja watched as the brothers dropped the swords and gave a good hug to each other before falling to the ground, worn out. The crowd might not have been too happy about it, but she couldn't hide the smile.

"Now that it's over would you like to each claim your kiss? That's if the ladies are interested in taking the tie." Marcus boomed again, pointing a finger for Sonja and Layla to come to the center of the grandstand. The girls left their bags with John as the brothers crawled off the ground. They stripped of the chain mail handing it to the squires who had taken their other armor. They climbed the stairs on either side of the girls. Layla was looking at Kale with anticipation, while Sonja tried to hide the smile from Nick.

"Sonja."

She turned to meet his eyes still trying to contain the smile.

"Nick?"

"Do I get a kiss?"

"You didn't win, you tied." She heard the crowd cheer as Layla kissed Kale, but it didn't distract her from her own knight, his lips, his eyes.

"You want me to go back to beating on my brother?"

She felt a hand on her back push her, landing in Nick's arms.

"Kiss me, Sonja."

It was what she wanted, what they both wanted. A fear in her boiled up that he would go even more overboard with protecting her. Being so close to him though, after the way her heart reacted all day, she couldn't stop herself.

She pushed her lips against his, just long enough for his breath to catch somewhere in his chest, his arms going weak giving her a chance to wiggle free.

Heading back to pick up her packages, she could feel her body going flush, and her eyes getting hazy.

It was only a second, but it would have to do. Her lips against his were worth the pain of the day. He savored it watching her walk away.

With so many people watching their first true display of affection, how could they have known one would loss his last bit of hold on sanity?

Sonja bent down making sure to give Nick more to look at, until her eye caught him in the crowd.

Nick rushed past her, the fatherly tone yelling back, "Stay here."

"Nick, don't." He was already down the stairs, Kale only a few steps behind him. She grabbed the sword out of her bag, knowing that neither brother had one on him, leaving the dwindling crowd confused. And Layla with Marcus and John.

She lost them in the crowd. Gunfire echoed. She rushed toward the sound, while others—screaming—rushed away. They made an opening for her, afraid as much of her sword as a gun. Her heart pounding, holding back the tears, her dreams flashing through her mind with panicked possible scenarios of who got shot and where.

Jerry was aiming the gun toward Nick and Kale again as he ran away, Kale was sitting on the ground, holding his arm.

"I can't believe the bastard shot me."

Sonja had the advantage of surprise coming out of the crowd right next to Jerry, she hit his wrist with the sword, before the trigger could be pulled again, the gun flying away. She pulled her sword back to her, noticing the blood on the blade. Shock rushed over her as Jerry disappeared into the crowd.

"Sonja!" Kale brought her back to reality as Nick ran past her, taking the sword from her as he gave chase. Detective Ivan ran past her other side, picking up the discarded gun on his way.

Wanting to go after Nick, to make him stop before the day could turn worse. The memory of Jerry pointing the gun at two people she loved more than she ever felt for him. The fire inside her was growing.

She knelt down to Kale, "Are you okay?"

"Can you believe he shot me?"

Sonja ripped his shirt open, amazed that she could hold her stomach as blood trickled down his arm.

"You aren't going to pass out on me?"

"Not yet." She replied, making a bandage out of his shirt, counting her heartbeats.

"He will be fine. Jerry is running scared." Kale added with a wince as she tightened the makeshift bandage around his arm.

A woman, whom Kale recognized as Agnes, the weapon smith's wife, dropped two swords next to them. "You all might need these about now."

Nick slowed as he got to the end of the crowd, looking back behind him, Jerry nowhere in sight. Detective Ivan caught up to him, pointed him one-way around the crowd, while he talked into his radio moving the other way.

Nick slowly walked through the crowd, looking for any sign of him. As he came back around to where Sonja was helping Kale with his wound, his heart shuddered with the thought he could have lost either of them. "You okay, Kale?"

"Yeah." He put his hand over the bandage as Sonja's stood.

"Don't you ever go chasing after someone like that, you are lucky he didn't get a better shot and kill one of you instead of only clipping Kale." The fire in her eyes was taking over.

Nick wanted to be sorry for it. But he wasn't.

Kale jumped in with a laugh in his voice, "Really I am fine. I'd like to get to a hospital and quit bleeding, but I'll live."

The detective tried to break up the argument, too, "Lost him, officers are already searching the cars as they leave. She's right. You boys are lucky."

"I'm glad you stuck around, Detective." Nick shook the man's hand.

"I assumed he wanted to watch as his guy grabbed her, to bring her to him. I'm guessing when we foiled that plan he was going to give up for the day until he saw her kiss you."

Sonja sat burying her head in her lap, and started to cry. She had caused this all.

"Whose blood is on the sword?" The detective continued.

"Jerry's, she got a good slice of him when he tried to take another shot at us." Nick said.

"She is doing good at protecting herself, and you too."

"Proud of her." Nick said.

She could hear, he wasn't so proud of himself. Through the tears, she managed to eke out, "What did you expect me to do? My heart was racing, and Kale was bleeding."

Nick reached down and helped her up. As sirens of an ambulance got closer, he pulled her close and whispered to her: "If that bastard got upset over a kiss, I'll give him something to be upset over."

"Why can't we just get him out of our lives?"

"Because, as long as you are happy and healthy, I'm afraid he won't stop. I'd rather drive him to do something stupid, that's when we will catch him."

Sonja buried her head in his good shoulder, as they followed the detective who was helping Kale to the ambulance.

12.

They left the hospital, almost two hours later, with a drugged Kale passed out in the back of his truck. Sonja drove home since Nick's shoulder looked like her face had a few weeks before. She did surprisingly well driving the horse trailer, even though she didn't try to back it into its place. The brothers were giving her all kinds of new experiences.

Nick half carried Kale to his room, with Sonja trying her best to help. They dropped him on the bed, careful of the bandages on his arm. Then they unloaded the horses, brushed them down, and made sure they had enough food and water. Nick's bow was never more than a foot away. Silently they moved Nick's car and Kale's truck to the back of the house before locking down the house.

Sonja drew a steaming bath, not intending it for herself. Her mind was racing and had been. What did Nick mean by he would give Jerry something to be upset over?

The living room was dark. Nick stood looking out the front window as an officer passed by the window. "Nick?"

"Yes Sonja?"

"I drew you a bath and I'm sorry about today." Her voice was broken, the fire out for now.

"Why? You didn't cause it."

"Yes, I did. If I hadn't fought back, if I hadn't left, if I hadn't come here…"

"You would be miserable—if you were alive. There is no place we would rather you be."

"I can go home to Memphis, he wouldn't chase me that far."

"Yes he would. You just wouldn't have us to protect you there."

"It would be safer for everyone, at least that's what I think."

Nick turned away from the window to see her standing in the middle of the living room, staring at the floor with her arms crossed. He had never seen her so closed off. His hand skimmed across her chin as he gently lifted her eyes up to his. The hurt in her caused his heart to beat within his chest as if wanting to get out and wrap her in love.

"Sonja, you belong here. It might have taken three years, and running from him, but you know its true."

"Kale got shot today, if I wasn't here that wouldn't have happened. It could have just as easily been you. It could have been more than…"

He tried his best to keep his voice calm and steady with the mixture of emotions boiling within him. "You think Kale is worried about his arm? Or was worried about it? He was worried about you, and me. You were right. I shouldn't have taken after the bastard. If I hadn't Kale wouldn't have been behind me when I ducked."

Her heart dropped lower still, which—until it did—she didn't think conceivable. The possibilities playing in her thoughts were excruciating. The bullet could have easily gone through both of them, leaving her alone. She cried again as he led her upstairs to the bathroom.

Nick closed the door as far as he felt safe in

doing so, he didn't want the light to disturb Kale, nor the door to keep him from hearing anything in the house.

"If you want to feel bad about something, you can help me off with this shirt, so I can get in the bath." Nick said as he tried to remove his shoes.

She caught him as he lost his balance.

"Sit down before you fall over."

He sat on the commode, watching as she took off his shoes and socks. "I could get used to service like this."

She smiled, too lost in thought to come back with an intelligent response, let alone something witty. Offering her hand to help him, she stood up. Her fingers wrapped around the button of his pants and he grabbed her hand.

Nervously explaining, "Maybe I should do that."

"Why? Are you afraid to be naked in front of me?"

He was definitely afraid of something. Before this day, she wasn't sure that fear was even a possibility for him. She caught the glimpse of his eyes before he realized his brother's wound was minimal. The look was absolute fear that his brother was gone, stripped from his life.

"Afraid? No."

"Worried I'm going to be embarrassed?"

The more his voice fluctuated the more she kept hers constant.

"You . . . No." His voice was unsure, his mind pushing him where he wasn't ready to go, pushing him to take her. To whisper his heart to her.

"What would you have to be ashamed of?"

"The fact that you excite me enough that I can't

help . . ." He didn't want to come out and say it, hoping instead she would get the point.

"Why would that be shameful?"

The thought alone made him close his eyes tightly. Having seen her naked in his bathroom made the thoughts worse. He found he was losing the battle to control himself, but managed to find control over his voice again.

"Sonja... I don't think you are ready for what I have to say."

She didn't want only his body after today, at least not right now. She wanted his heart, wanted him to touch her, especially after what he said downstairs. He was right, there was no place she belonged except right where she was.

"Open your eyes, look at me, and say that."

The deep breath came as he opened his eyes, staring straight into hers. They showed the pain of the day, the anguished caused by Jerry.

"Not everything in my life is solely up to you, Nick."

"I'm still gonna tell you if I think it would be a mistake."

"You think *we* could be a mistake?" Her heart stopped.

"Never." Nick shook his head, realizing the meanings behind that one word answer, "But I think rushing into anything would be."

"How is me helping you to undress to get in a bathtub, rushing?"

"The urges you arouse in me by doing that— that's rushing."

"Why do we have to have such intelligent conversations? They might be to the point, but still too intelligent and not enough emotion."

"Because I wouldn't want you to call me a 'pig'."

That simple fact brought the smile back to her face.

"Will you let me help you now?"

He let her hands slip out of his, she pulled off his shirt worried if she went after the pants he would stop her again. He pulled her close as his shirt hit the floor, her face lying against his bare chest. She heard how breathless her voice sounded as his name escaped her lips. She needed to know what he was thinking, what he was feeling.

"Give me a minute before you do anything else." The feel of her sent chills through his body, he knew it was too soon. He knew she wasn't ready for his heart. But if she pushed, he would blurt it out. All three years of emotions, of thoughts, of memories, right at the tip of his tongue—if he would just let it out.

If he wasn't careful she would get hurt where she was most precious, her heart. After all, her heart attracted him to her above all else. The way she treated people. The way she trusted everyone, even Jerry. It never hurt that she was beautiful, smart, and funny.

He pulled himself together with the thought that no matter what, he had a great friend in her. Even that worried him. She was a friend he would miss beyond compare if the relationship didn't work out. That alone would keep him under control, until she told him otherwise. He let his arms slip down her body, simply enjoying the feel of her. Even though his hands no longer held her in place, she stayed against his chest, as she gently swayed side to side.

The sound of his heart was peaceful, it showed how alive he was, and would remain. It was strong, and steady, just like the body that encased it. She could imagine sleeping curled up next to him, his bare chest against her, his heart singing her to sleep. His whispering of her name brought her back from the lullaby.

"Sonja."

"Nick?"

"Our bath is getting cold, darlin'."

"Our?"

"Yes, I need someone to work out the knots in my back I got from fighting for a kiss—from someone who someday may give them to me freely."

"You would have fought today, even if my lips weren't part of the prize. You have a problem with me helping you out of our pants, but not to be in a bathtub with me naked?"

"I'm under control again."

"Why do you need to be in control?"

"Honestly?" His voice sounded partly mad, the father tone was back.

She pulled away from his chest to look in his eyes. "Always."

"I need to be in control, because I refuse to hurt you, or to push you, especially after today. I will wait and so will you."

Sonja knew he meant that he could wait until she was ready for more, much more than a 'romp'. She slid her hand to his waist, and popped the button, then slid down the zipper, watching his eyes as they intensified, growing darker, fluttering as she touched him.

"Sonja, behave." He was getting excited again, he was trying to keep a straight face, trying to keep his mind on their friendship, not on the possibility of a sexual interaction.

His pants slid to the floor. As she pulled her

shirt over her head, he closed his eyes again. She was thankful for the privacy as she quickly removed the rest of her clothes and slid into the bath.

He opened his eyes again when he heard the water slosh, finding her chest deep in the bubbles, her own eyes closed tight.

He slid his boxers down and climbed in the tub in front of her. He felt her breath catch as his back pressed lightly against her. He could feel her heart accelerate, and her racing blood quickly warmed her skin.

"Sonja?"

"Give me a minute," whispered from of her parted lips as he started to move forward. "No! Don't move, just . . . stay."

She wrapped her legs around him as he lay back against her again. This time her body shuddered as his pressed against hers, his hands gently rubbing across her legs.

His aching muscles were enjoying the hot water, as his body enjoyed the caress of hers.

"Let me know if I am hurting you, darlin'."

Her eyes opened at the use of that endearment, she repeated it with a dreamy, breathy sound, "Darling?"

"No, darlin'."

He liked the way she said it as well, but couldn't help but say it to her again. It was the one word close to "I love you," that he could say without needing to hear "I love you" back. His heart stopped as he felt her lips against his shoulder, the tenderness and love from that single touch, sent his brain to another world.

She was not sure why she did it, even as she did. Maybe it was that he was worried about hurting her or that he was so relaxed against her or the word "darlin'" or the bruise on his shoulder that she had caused. But something definitely told her to kiss him. She started for his neck, but decided instead to kiss his shoulder because of the pain she had caused him there over the past few days. She assumed her choice was a good one when his chest shook.

"Sonja?"

"Yes, Nick."

"Maybe we should keep our lips to ourselves."

"You are the one that fought all day for a simple kiss. Now you want me to keep my lips to myself? That would be a mixed message, darling." She kissed his shoulder again as her hands wrapped around his chest.

He found himself defenseless against her. He wanted her to stop, to keep their embraces from going any further. Yet at the same time he didn't want her to stop at all—so it would go even farther. If she wanted to know about mixed messages, she needed to spend some time in his brain.

"Where else do you hurt, Nick?"

"Right now I can't feel anything but you."

Sonja wrapped her arms around him tighter, feeling safer than she had in her entire life. She marveled at the feel of his chest as it moved erratically in and out, she was causing that, just by being so close.

Jerry hadn't been a bad lover, as far as she knew, because he had also been her only. She remembered someone telling her at some point that no matter what happens in life, that first one is special. She assumed that was one of the reasons she had stayed so long. Her heart didn't like the thought of jumping into just any bed. Her imagination played the scene again of her and Nick rolling around in his bed. She figured she was overplaying the possibility, too much Hollywood in her imagination. But someday she would find out for sure.

Sonja was torn from her daydream by the sound of one word, "Nick!" It resonated, deep and scared, and it came from Kale's room. Nick jumped out of the bathtub not worried about her seeing him excited and naked anymore. He pulled on his boxers, while his body was still half wet, and she was wrapping her bathrobe around her. She was right behind him all the way to Kale's room.

Kale was still half drugged, facing the door with his shoulder propped on several pillows as his brother came through the open door. The relief on Kale's face explained a lot.

Still Nick had asked, "Bad dream, brother?"

"Yeah. You didn't duck."

"Thanks for the thought, but I'm the one that's fine. How are you doing otherwise?" He asked as he sat on the bed.

"Need a drink, bad."

Nick turned to ask Sonja to grab something, she was already heading down the stairs.

"Did I disturb the two of you?"

"Na. Just enjoying a hot bath."

"Together?"

He didn't know if he wanted to tell Kale, afraid he would be upset or sorry for interrupting them. Still he knew Kale would watch their entire life to some degree. He might as well know.

"Yes, together."

Sonja came back up the stairs, carrying a large glass of ice tea. The conversation stopped her dead.

"She's not ready for love." Kale said softly.

Her heart skipped a beat, he was right to some degree. For Nick though she would give every ounce of love she had within her.

"I will give her all she can take until she is ready for more."

"I would tread very lightly."

"I'm doing my best, Kale." His soft voice was almost sad. "You don't need to worry about it right now. You just need to heal."

"I could be on my death bed and I would worry about the two of you. Just don't want ya'll to screw up my life in the process of falling in love." Even drugged Kale's wit was remarkable.

"Selfish aren't you?"

When they laughed she decided it would be a good time to come into the room.

"Ah, a vision with something cold to drink." Kale warned his brother as she came in the door.

Sonja and Nick helped Kale to sit up as he drank, then Nick left the room to get a new bandage for Kale's arm. Sonja took the opportunity to talk to Kale, alone.

"How are you really?"

"Hurts like hell. As much from the competition as from the gunshot."

"When you feel up to it, I will draw you a bath too."

"As long as you don't join me in it. I'd like you to save that honor for Nick."

"I can agree to that. You're really alright with all this?"

"It's been comin' for a long time, even if you were blind to it. Someday I hope I can call you 'sister' with a new meaning. Just don't rush it." Kale was smiling, hoping he was making sense. The drugs were affecting his mind a bit. His eyes were closed, simply because he couldn't keep them open, but he could feel her lips press against his forehead.

"Thank you, Kale. Maybe tomorrow I'll call Layla to come play nurse."

"Layla . . . You okay with that?" His voice went soft as he asked.

"I think it's wonderful. Two people I love as much as you and her, being together. What could go wrong?"

"Depends on the two people. Sonja please, don't hurt him."

The thought of hurting Nick was a weight great enough to crush her. Hurting anyone would, except Jerry, but Nick even more so than her own flesh and blood.

Kale decided to save her from her own torment. "How about another drink while we wait on him."

She helped him to sit up again and drink as Nick came in the room. The three enjoyed a little mindless conversation while Nick carefully changed his brothers dressing, only causing a few grimaces. They helped Kale off with his pants, and Sonja tucked him in his blankets, before leaving his room.

She started down the hall toward the bathroom as Nick grabbed her robe, pulling her back to him and his arms.

"You need to go to bed and get some rest." Nick whispered so he wouldn't disturb Kale.

"It's okay, I'm not sure I can sleep. I will take this watch, you can have the next."

"I know I can't sleep." He was moving his hands unconsciously up and down her arms. "How about, you lay down in your bed, I'll take my chair out of the library to your room so I can watch out the window."

"Not bad. Why don't you lay in my bed with me? I really don't want you to be very far away." She remembered how safe she felt with him in the tub.

"I guess we can do that. As long as you sleep some and most of all behave."

"I will try."

She said trying her best to look innocent. Nick let his hands fall from her body, turning toward his room.

"That's the wrong way. I know I don't bother you so much that you lost your sense of direction."

"Yes, you do but if I am going to be in the same bed as you and not . . . " His mind pushed all the images of what they could do. He chose to shake his head with the small nervous laugh escaping. "I need pajamas. And so do you."

Sonja couldn't help but laugh as she went to the bathroom and drained the water from the tub. She picked up the dirty clothes from the room. She met him in the hallway, handing over his dirty clothes, before going to her room with hers.

He came back to find her just slipping out of the robe, her back turned towards the door as she dressed again in pajama bottoms and a tank top. He couldn't help but watch. She was elegant, sexy, and driving him out of his mind, but he loved every minute of it and every bit of her. The silhouette of her body was almost more erotic than the full frontal view in the bathroom.

The same force that caused him to know she was around without seeing her came over Sonja as well. She could feel his eyes move along her skin so she took extra time in pulling back on her clothing before letting him know she knew he was there. "You know you could knock when entering my room."

"My house, therefore my room. And what would be the fun in knocking? I have something for you too."

"A surprise?" Her voice was chipper and lush.

"Something I think you will like." He moved to where there was less than a foot between them and handed her the bag. "Sorry haven't had time to wrap it's been a busy day."

She smiled as she pulled the newspaper-wrapped item out of the bag. It was heavy. She unwrapped it slowly. She watched his excitement grow as he wondered if she would enjoy the present. As it dropped out of the paper into her hand, she recognized one of the candlesticks that she had decided not to buy. "You followed me this morning."

"Had to! After all, I was still worried about your safety."

Her eyes fluttered as his hand brushed her hair from her face.

"Thank you."

"Thank you for the sword."

"It is nice isn't it?"

"You did well in picking all three out."

"I also made the appointment for your car Monday."

"I know."

He watched as she sat the candlesticks on her dresser in the middle of the pictures of her nieces and nephews. It was, he knew, a special spot.

He continued to watch as she glided to the bed and pulled down the covers. Covers that would soon be draped across their bodies, together. She slid her legs under the covers propping herself up with her elbows.

"Are you going to stand there or come join me?" Her voice was shaky, and her body began to quiver as he started to walk across the room. He stopped halfway to the bed. He seemed to find something interesting on the floor for a moment before turning his eyes back to her.

"I'm not sure about this," he finally said as he stared at her, watching her smile return.

"You are welcome to get the chair out of the library if you want to." Her voice had returned to normal. She was aware he was as nervous as she was. She found herself wanting to feel him inside her as much as wanting to wait for the perfect time. Him standing without a shirt on in her room was not helping her mind any.

Nick ran across the rest of the room jumping onto her bed, then over on top of her. Her body froze as his connected with her until he started to tickle her.

"Are you trying to kick me out of your bed before I get in it?"

She couldn't answer from laughing so hard, elated that he wasn't as serious as normal. He finally quit tickling her. Her eyes opened to find the serious Nick back. She could only shake her head and close her eyes, knowing he continued to stare at her.

His serious side pulled on her heart as much as anything about him. It made him honest, trustworthy. As long as he actually would tell you instead of keeping it held inside, you knew exactly what he was thinking. Then he would come across the room and tickle the life out of someone just to show that things were too serious. Even for him.

Nick moved to the other side of the bed and slipped under the covers. He wasn't sure how long he could resist his growing desire to push himself upon her if he kept staying so close to her. He rested his head against the pillow, looking over her out the window. As she rolled to her side, matching the way he was laying, he slid to her body, pulling her closer. He rested his chin on her shoulder, whispering. "Good night, darlin'."

"Good night, Nick."

Nick danced her around the backyard. They laughed silently, enjoying each other. She had on a beautiful sundress and no shoes, he wore a button up shirt, and slacks, like he wore most of the time, and they just kept spinning. Then, though there was no noise, he stopped suddenly. He fell to his knees, a trickle of blood coming from his mouth, and then collapsed to the ground. Jerry stood behind him, gun held high.

She gasped for air but didn't scream as she sat up in the bed, sweat covering her body. She was alone in the bed. Her heart settled down when she heard laughter echoing down the hall. No noise in her life ever sounded so good, she put her head back on the pillow and cried.

She knew in her heart that if anything happened to either of them she would never forgive herself. She knew that even this house couldn't fully protect them from an obsessed lunatic. He wanted her. He would get her and take out anyone in his way.

The plan formed in her mind as she dried the tears from her eyes.

She ran down the hall, into Kale's room surprising both the brothers that she was even awake. Jumping over Kale's legs she bounced on the bed until she was facing them. They laughed even louder. The smile on her face was exciting and contagious.

"Lets leave."

"Say what?"

Each of them, still smiling, looked confused.

"Leave, go some where, vacation. I can get off duty cops to watch the house. We can just go for a week. Let them find Jerry, throw his ass in prison."

"Where would we go? And why." Nick thought her last gasket had just blown.

"Who cares! Up to Memphis, over to Atlanta, hell we can fly and be anywhere but here."

The looks hurt, she was trying to be as serious as possible.

"You think hiding will work?" Doubt worked its way from Nick's voice to her veins.

"If it can keep him away for a week, let Kale heal and let the police do their jobs without putting your lives in jeopardy. Then yes."

The fire was working its way through her eyes, Nick was beginning to find that irresistible.

Kale nodded in agreement that it wasn't a bad idea. Next time he saw Jerry he wanted him to be in a hospital bed, in an orange county jump suit, or at the other end of his fist, which would send him to one of the other two places. Still he wasn't sure what he was capable of with a chunk missing out of his arm.

Nick on the other hand, the usual voice of reason, voiced his opposing opinion. "What's to say if we leave he won't follow us or have us followed. Then attack in another state. That would be worse than if it happened right here. We all have jobs to go to that we love."

He knew that none of their jobs would be lost if they just up and left but everything else was valid. Plus, he wanted a piece of Jerry, he didn't want to leave the law to do it all.

"You would rather stay and let him get another lucky shot in than disappear for a week . . . or two?"

"I'm not running from that little worm."

"No, I am and I'm taking you with me."

No one was laughing or smiling anymore.

"I think we should go. That's if I'm still

invited." Kale piped in trying to get someone to smile or laugh.

Instead he got two stern looks.

"If we run and they don't catch him then we still have the same issue. He wants you and he will not stop until he has you or is behind bars or dead."

"If they do catch him its over. The detective won't let him out of jail again."

The loud knock echoing through the house made her jump and everyone go quiet. Nick silently moved to the window to see the detective's car setting in the driveway. He bounded down the stairs hoping for good news, anything good. Sonja came down slower, helping Kale since the handrail was on the wrong side and the pain pill—twice the regular dosage, was making him groggy.

Nick flung open the door, and spoke to the detective as if he was a dear and old friend, "Please tell me you have good news."

The detective's face said he didn't. Instead he thought of something good, and started there, "Well, you still have a chance to kill him?"

"I'll take it."

"Miss Mitchell." The detective nodded her way.

"Good morning, Detective. You keep odd hours."

It was, after all, only six in the morning.

"No rest for the wicked. I have a lot to say. Hold the questions for the end. Do you want sugar coated or straight?"

Scanning from Nick to Kale then back to the detective, she said, "Straight please."

Nick's arms wrapped around her waist pulling her to his lap as he sat on the end of the couch. Something in his heart said this was going to be a bad morning.

"Straight," The detective paused while she shook her head. "We found his car at the fair, it's in impound, some weird stuff in it. Pictures of Sonja, some taken since she left him, some from right here at this house. Ties, handcuffs, tortuous things by nature."

Nick could feel Sonja start to shake. He held her tighter, gently kissing her back. Nick couldn't help but wonder if Jerry had tortured her before or if that was a new part of his game.

"We have no idea where he is at the moment but we know where he was at around three this morning." The detective took a deep breath before he continued.

"I think I am going to throw up." Sonja said, with her eyes on the floor.

Nick squeezed her tighter careful to not squeeze her ailing stomach. He felt her grabbing his arms for dear life.

"He broke into Ms. McKenzie's apartment..."

Sonja jumped out of Nick's arms making a mad dash up the stairs. They all heard as her knees hit the bathroom floor.

"The girl is going to be fine. She got in enough hits on him and called the police, he went running out of the apartment, bleeding himself. She said she ripped the bandage off his arm where Sonja cut him with the sword and pushed her fingernails into it. Her hands were still covered with blood when the officers arrived. We're sure it was him."

They watched as Sonja carefully came back down the stairs, when she was halfway, she took a hard seat on the steps.

"Sonja, he said she will be fine." Nick said.

"How bad?"

"A few cuts and bruises, really not worse than

you when I first met you. We did take her to the hospital just to have everything checked out. Asked me to make sure and get it through to you that she is fine."

"Sonja is she someone you work with?" Nick posed the question that she hadn't decided to answer yet.

"You don't know the name?" The detective was completely confused now.

Sonja rested her eyes on Kale, she could see the anger well in him as he realized who Ms. McKenzie was.

"He couldn't get us, knowing we would all protect each other. So he went after Layla."

Nick looked at Detective Ivan. He wanted blood. He wanted Jerry's blood. "What is the best way we can set the bastard up?"

"I'm an officer of the law, son. I can't conspire to set up anyone. I can say he is most likely to strike when she is alone and most vulnerable."

Sonja's voice was stronger, she knew what Nick was thinking, and she wasn't going to stop him. "So everyone goes to work, and I wait. He'll think it's a trap. We have to sell it well."

"We will, darlin'."

13.

Sonja started making calls as soon as the detective left. She called Jack first, explaining he would have to do a week without either of them. The crash from his end of the phone expressed it all. She asked that he call everyone and alert them that they could be a target, since they even knew her. She called her sisters, each again pleading that she come home to them. Without explaining, she told them the answer was still no. She told them as well to keep the kids close and she would call when it was over. *If I don't call someone will.* She almost changed her plans.

Nick and Kale took turns talking to their mother and then the rest of the family, asking them to be careful. Trying to explain as little of the situation as they could, neither mentioning Kale's gunshot wound.

Sonja called the airline, booked a ticket for Layla to the Virgin Islands, knowing she always wanted to go but would never take the vacation on her own.

After a lot of convincing Kale took a ticket too, three days on an island watching Layla didn't seem like a bad vacation to him. He was of little use to his loved ones while he was injured. He packed a bag, said his goodbyes, and left to pick Layla up at the hospital.

Nick and Sonja spent the rest of the day arming the house; hiding swords, knives, and bows throughout. Anywhere she could possibly be and need a weapon, one was concealed. Nick nailed the back screen shut and attached a second latch on the front one. When

Sonja ran out of things to do, she started to clean. When Nick ran out of things to do, he started to cook dinner. They kept the lights low giving lots of shadows for someone to hide in.

They lit candles for dinner, sitting as close to each other as they could with music gently playing in the background. Never in their lives had it just been the two of them alone for more than an hour. They really didn't know what to do other than stare at each other and try to make small talk. Anything to avoid the questions in their minds and hearts. Their hearts were growing closer by the second, whether they thought it was time or not.

When dinner was finished, they did the dishes and cleaned up the kitchen together, laughing and smiling, even when nothing was said. Each enjoyed the gentle touch, as they passed by, a delicate kiss when the moment seemed right. Everything was moving along better than a movie script.

When the kitchen was clean to his satisfaction, he led her to the living room, let the light come on dimly, and pulled her close. They swayed to the music as he scanned the drape free windows for signs of life.

Her dream from the night before stayed in her mind through the day. As long as she kept busy she didn't think too hard about the possible ways that Jerry might get the better of her or Nick or both. She had wanted Kale to stay for the extra hands and eyes but knew he would be safer far away. And knew they could plan better without him.

Jerry had three days to strike before Layla and Kale came home. She hoped he would take the bait: her. Even with the thoughts of everything that could go wrong, she couldn't help but enjoy their displays of affection. If Jerry didn't like the small kiss he had spied at the end of the competition, he would hate the things they had three days to show him. He was pushing them closer together instead of pulling her away.

They danced for hours in the living room, having a great time of it. Laughing at each other when they missed a beat, smiling as their bodies mixed together.

"Are you ready to go up stairs, darlin'?"

"Did we ever decide which bed to sleep in?" she whispered back, sure if anyone was listening they wouldn't hear.

"Depends if we can actually sleep."

He lifted her chin and met her eyes with his, which he left wide open as their lips touched. She tried to keep her eyes open, her lashes fluttering as he gently skimmed her lips with his. He pressed against her a little more. If something went wrong in their plan, he didn't want to miss anything about her. He wanted to memorize every bit of her body, knowing he would never love again.

He wrapped his arms around her, pulling her body tight against his as her lips parted and invited him to kiss her more.

He took the invitation as did she, each pushing further, knowing they didn't want to stop, knowing they might not be able to. He slowly pulled her lips from his, lightly kissing them again. His head swam with images of her that he saved over three years, as he added the feel and smell of her in the here and now to those memories. He pulled her off the floor, wrapping her in his arms to carry her upstairs.

"Nick." She whispered, still breathless from the emotions pouring through her.

"Just going upstairs, darlin'." He whispered before kissing her. He slowly carried her up the flight of stairs and down the hallway to his bed. He sat her on the end of it, not sure how to proceed. She swayed to a beat in her head as he removed her shirt. With her eyes still closed, he opened the window and removed his shirt. Carefully scanning the backyard.

He hoped the cool air from the window would help keep him alert to the present. As he knelt down in front of her, he realized that hope was only a dream. She could warm him in a blizzard.

He whispered again so only she could hear, "Sonja, tell me . . ." *Tell me you love me, tell me you want me, tell me to stop,* coursed through his mind as he kissed her neck sliding the two of them across his bed to lay her head on a pillow.

She could hardly hear anything above the pounding of her heart. Her skin aware of every touch, of every kiss, of every caress. Her heart wanted to scream, wanted to tell him everything that scared her, and everything she wanted of him. His name was the only thing she could get out of her mouth between gasping for air. So many sensations were taking over her body that she couldn't form enough thought to speak anything but his name. So, she spoke just that, softly, over and over. The pillow under her head didn't bring her to her senses anymore. Everything in her body said to keep on the same course, don't slow down, just jump in with both feet, and forget about looking. Until his voice, reminding her of her dreams, pulled her back to reality.

His body pressed against hers, his lips slowly taking her skin. She could feel he had no sense of urgency, that he was enjoying everything about her, which only caused her heart to pound all the more.

"Nick . . ." Finally came out of her lips, loud enough for them both to hear. He pulled his body away from hers, taking deep breaths. He leaned to kiss her lips. He stopped himself. Irresistibly, he tried once more before he flopped to the other side of the bed.

He pulled off the rest of his clothing with a new sense of urgency then rolled over, smiling at her as he removed hers. Her own smile met his, knowing she could stop them if she needed too. Either way he was back in control of himself or he would have been serious instead of smiling at her.

Even with no pressure of actually having intercourse, they moved as if they would. Whispering in each other's ears to keep them alert instead of drifting off into the pleasure again. The bedspread, she kept over his back, the sheet he kept between their bodies.

"Nick is this going too far?"

"We want him to lose it, to do something stupid. If I was him and you were in his bed, that would do it. We already know the soft kiss yesterday drove him crazy. This just might kill him without me having to touch him."

"I like that thought." He kissed her neck again, she wrapped her legs around his. He stopped moving, resting his body on hers.

"I don't think I can take this anymore." He said still whispering in her ear. "I'm going to pay dearly for this already."

"Kale left specific instructions for me not to hurt his brother."

"Only one way to stop that and you are not ready."

"We need to stay alert."

"That too. We already came close to blocking out the world once."

"Our conversation is too intellectual again, Nick." She laughed, "We could be on a plane to the islands first thing in the morning. Forget that anyone else exists on the planet."

He moved to where he could see her face. She was serious. "Sonja you talk like that and send me to another planet. I want more than anything to lose myself in you."

"Then say it."

"You're not . . ."

"Don't tell me when I am ready." The fire was in her voice, not just her eyes. "I stopped before because I worry about him coming here when we are preoccupied, too lost in each other to hear or see it coming."

"I have that same concern, but not as much as I have for you, for your heart."

She couldn't help but let the tear glide out. Nothing before in her life had ever been so from the heart, or driven hers so far. She couldn't do anything to stop it, while he begged her not to cry. His lips catching each tear as it fell alone.

"Nick, I . . ."

"Don't!" He said it hard as he wrapped his arms around her. Taking deep breaths, he whispered again. "If . . . if this goes bad . . . I'm not sure I can live knowing . . . what you are thinking."

"I want to scream it. I want to . . . make sure that bastard, knows he can't have me. That my heart is no longer mine to give. It is yours." She felt his body shake as he took her lips. It wasn't the carefree kiss of when they were playing, it wasn't the romance when they were dancing. It was passion and urgency.

The words rang through his brain, "It is yours." Three years and three words meant more to him than, anyone, even her saying "I love you." "It is yours." There was a possession of the soul that came with it, a possession of her heart. Every second of every feeling he had for her rushed through him.

Her body curled around his while their lips spoke their language. The noise brought them quickly back to reality. Something outside snapped. A branch, a twig, something. Someone. Nick pulled back meeting her wild eyes. He jumped up on the bed, pulling on his pants then gently placing his feet on the floor. Not taking his eyes off the open window, he grabbed the bow. *If this is Jerry,* he thought, *I might have missed my opportunity to tell her.* He backed up to the bed, sat on the edge pulling her to him, kissing her as the tears rolled down her face. "I love you. Darlin'."

He let her slip from his arms and jumped out the window, to the oak tree.

Grabbing the pajama bottoms and tank top, they had stashed, and the sword under them her brain started doing laps. She locked the bedroom door and stood ready at the window, then waited. Shock was the first thing that came to mind. The shock of the reality that he just left her to chase down Jerry. Shock that he just said the one thing he wasn't sure he wanted to say, the one thing he had resisted saying for so long. Shock that she didn't know how to convey that she felt the same. She wiped away the tears without letting up her grip on the sword.

With her emotions in control of her body, Sonja couldn't help but jump when his voice yelled from the backyard. "Come let me in."

She unlocked the bedroom door, throwing it open as she ran down the stairs to the front door. Unlocking the front door, the thought crossed her mind that there were to many obstacles in her way. She swung it open, unlocked both latches on the screen and rushed onto the porch. He pushed the sword down with his bow until it hit the porch. He wrapped his free arm around her, passionately taking her lips.

The sword clunked as it hit the porch. She wanted both hands to touch him with, to make sure he was real and unharmed. The tears stopped as he pulled her off the ground lavishing her with kisses.

"Would it have been better to not know, darlin'?"

"No, I already knew. I never want to keep anything from you, don't keep anything from me."

"It was only the neighbor's dog."

"Like the detective said, he wants me alone."

"That doesn't make me feel any better." He stated.

"Lets go inside. I think we have given him enough if he's watching the front instead of the back."

"Then lets go to the back and give more."

She smiled picking up the sword, leading the way back inside.

Nick stopped inside the door, looking around outside. He wondered if Jerry was out there, glad she didn't know the neighbors didn't have a dog. He latched both locks then the door as she went up the stairs. He searched each room on his way back to bed making sure no one snuck in while they were on the porch. When he was satisfied, he found her under the covers naked again.

"You are gonna kill me yet."

"Wouldn't dream of it. You said lets give some more."

He dropped his pants and stepped out of them on his way. He slid in next to her pulling her to him without a sheet between them. "You do know what happens after a guy has sex?"

"Well the only other guy I know about would

leave for work."

"One, that's right." He kissed her neck, as his nerves started to eat at him. "He would leave, huh?"

"Yes." She said as her eyes rolled back, her brain tried to move, tried to stay in the room and not drift away again.

"Hmm, did he kiss you like this?"

Not that Nick cared how Jerry had kissed her, he wouldn't be doing it anymore. He did have other questions he needed answered.

"Never."

"Would he touch you, or just…"

"As little as possible."

"Hmm" She was being so honest, so open. He had his opportunity. "Did he ever torture you?"

"He kept me from you for three years. I consider that torture."

"So do I. But I was wondering about what the detective found in his car." His heart pounded as he waited for the answer, but he had to know. He couldn't look at her until she answered, choosing to kiss every inch of her skin within reach instead.

"No, nothing physical or sexual."

The deep breath of relief shook his body and pulled her from her mindless answering.

"Nick, that worried you?"

She used her hands that were playing with his hair to pull his face to hers, seeing a twinge of fear cross his eyes.

Nick's voice came out soft and slow, his words wouldn't form. "The thought of him hurting you. It was bad enough he left bruises on your face. Anything else, knowing you probably wouldn't have told us it hurt. I'm sorry I had to ask."

The smile that crossed her face was amazing to

him. So sweet and innocent, conveying emotions they each were having problems saying, that they kept bottled deep inside for so long. "You know about both times he ever harmed me."

Nick's eyes closed with the relief. "Emotionally?"

"I am a mess."

"You have a new fire about you. I don't think I've ever seen you angry, before the past few weeks."

"I don't remember being angry before."

"It looks good on you." He went back to kissing her neck.

"Nick . . ."

"Yes, darlin'?"

"What happens…?"

"Fall asleep or want more."

"Sounds good."

"Not tonight." She rolled her head, knowing he was right. Neither of them could afford for him to be dead to the world.

"Then we spend the night talking to each other."

"As long as I can keep touching you, kissing you, then that is the plan."

14.

They crawled out of bed the next morning, not tired, but in love even more. He shut the windows and locked them. They climbed into his shower together, amazed by each other's bodies, by touches.

When they got out, Nick again searched the house. She prepared their breakfast, he fixed his lunch. Staying as close as possible while he was still there.

She took her car, he took his, dropping it off at the dealership for a new window. She caught a ride back home with an off duty officer. Nick took her car and drove to work.

The officer let her out at the driveway and stayed until she was inside the house. She searched it thoroughly before sitting in the chair in the middle of the bottom floor, sword in hand, waiting. Her cell phone open with the detective's number ready to push send. She waited. She didn't move for lunch, she didn't move to close curtains. She waited, remembering his kisses. She waited, remembering his touch. She waited, remembering his love.

She didn't get tired, she hardly blinked. Her mind alone kept her from getting bored. They had whispered their plan. She knew what she had to do and how it would go. The planning was perfect. She just had to wait.

Anger fueled her as well. Kale getting shot . . . anger. Layla getting attacked . . . anger. Being near that bastard for three years and away from Nick . . . anger.

The thought of him touching her . . . anger. The thought of him watching her . . . anger.

At fifteen till four, she watched her car pull into the driveway and smiled for the first time since she left the car dealership that morning. But she didn't move. She watched as he rounded the house, and her smile grew. But she didn't move. He walked up on the porch. She rose from her chair, keeping the sword with her as she moved to the front door. He smiled from the other side. She unlocked the first one, opened it.

"Hello, darlin'." She unlocked the second door, twice, and opened it. Stepping out to the front porch, his arms wrapped around her waist, she wrapped hers around his neck.

"Be careful before you poke me with that." Nick said referring to the sword swinging behind him.

"I could say the same thing to you."

"I'm just happy you are looking at me and touching me."

"Let's go inside and do a little more of that."

He leaned down and kissed her, hoping someone was watching. Nick picked her up around the waist, pushing her backwards inside the door. When he let go of her lips, he turned and locked the screen then shut and locked the front door.

He turned to find her heading for the kitchen. "Didn't eat lunch did you?"

"No and it just hit me that I am famished. Want something while I'm in here?"

"You."

"Does that mean you missed me?" She pouted as he watched her fix a chicken salad sandwich.

"I missed you." He smiled, hoping at some point, he would never have to say that again.

She finished the sandwich, washed it down with

half a beer and then jumped up landing her bottom on the center island.

"Kiss me, Nick."

"What? You think I am at your beck and call?"

"You don't want to kiss me?"

"I didn't say that." He casually walked over to her, put one hand on the side of her, reached around, grabbed the beer, and walked out of the kitchen.

She watched as he sat in the chair she had occupied all day. She slid off the counter and walked into the dining room, around the table to stand in front of him.

Her eyes had the fire. As the first button of her shirt popped open, his ornery smile faded.

His eyes moving down with each button that came free from its hole. The fire within her grew.

He readjusted the way he was sitting as she dropped the shirt on the floor.

His eyes followed her hands back to the waist of her pants as she popped the button, and then unzipped them. He lost the last thread of sanity binding him.

She turned and faced the front door as she slid her pants down, then stepped out of them.

He marveled in the way her undergarments formed to her body as she turned around, black was a perfect color.

He watched as she preformed her best runway walk.

She took the beer away then stretched across him to place it on the table.

He kissed her stomach running his hands over the bare skin so close to his face.

She took a seat on his lap. "Will you ever deny me a kiss again?'"

"Never." His chest heaving with each arduous

breath, his heart pounding as if trying to escape.

"Then kiss me."

His hands grabbed at the cool skin on her back, as their lips met. Passion gripping them. Hearts pounding.

He couldn't take much of this after his day. Grabbing her bottom firm, he stood up, pulling her tighter against his chest. Carrying her upstairs, he dropped her on the bed and started pulling his pants off as she worked the buttons on the shirt. He turned around, shut and locked the bedroom door then opened the windows before turning back to the bed.

Sonja had no clue what he was doing, but willing to go with whatever he thought was best. She was having too much fun.

He climbed into the bed, sliding his boxers off as she helped him under the covers. He immediately removed her bra kissing down her body as he wiggled her underwear down her legs. He came up pressing his body on hers. It was her turn to look bewildered. He kissed across her neck, her cheek, finding her lips parted trying to find breath. He took them, softly as her fingers skimmed his back.

She was lost again, no thoughts, the only sound was their hearts rhythmic throbbing. He carefully pulled his lips from hers, wondering how they had already gotten this far. He wanted her, he wanted to hear her say it.

"Sonja, darlin'?" Nick skimmed his lips over hers without blocking them. Listening as a little sound came out with a breath.

"Nick . . . I am fine."

He took her lips, passion pouring out of him as he moved her to the top of their two-person pile, so that his hands were free to feel her body, which he did freely, without worrying about the weight of him hurting her. Each time their lips parted, he managed one word, "Sonja," before he was pushing at her lips again. At some point, he pulled her hair tie out causing her black waves to fall down around them.

He pulled her away, watching her face as she tried to breathe, "Sonja, talk to me, say something."

"More."

"I'm not sure I can take more?"

"Then take me."

He put her back on the bed looking in her eyes. Not being able to believe what she was saying. He had to be sure what she meant. "Sonja, I'm not sure . . ."

"I am." She interrupted him. "I do not want tomorrow to be the day that something goes wrong and you not know what I feel."

"I know you love me. I know that we feel the same. That will last me the rest of this life, whether it ends tomorrow or a hundred years from tomorrow."

She reached up and kissed him, he pulled back watching as the tears fell. It dawned on him that he had just put the thought of him dying in her brain, let alone dying tomorrow.

"Sonja I don't think fate is so cruel as to not let us be together."

"It has been for the past three years." She said with a nervous laughter.

"We won't let it any longer."

She wrapped her arms around him pulling him closer, kissing his neck. "That is why I love you."

Why? Because I don't back down, even from fate?"

"Because you say what I need. You do what I need. You always have. Except the fact I want you to make love to me and you refuse me. I don't want it to be show. I want to know you on every level. We have the friend thing down, and I could treat you like a brother. You could take over the role of my father and god knows I've acted like a spoiled brat at times. But I want to know you, every bit of you like I've never known anyone else."

"Intelligential conversation again. And I don't want to push you . . ."

"I am a big girl, been making my own decisions for years now. Most of them wrong when it comes to matters of the heart. I figure though *we* can't both be wrong."

"You are making this real hard on me."

"How so?"

"Because I want nothing more on this earth than you but I can't have you fully until you are one hundred percent positive."

She ran her mind over the past three years—mostly over the past year—and smiled. "I'm stupid is what this boils down to."

He started to talk. She put her fingers gently over his mouth.

"The last time I was here, I went back to Jerry because I was scared. Because he threatened you and Kale, and I couldn't take that. I went back, slept with him once in the past year and threw up after because he so sickened me." She lowered her eyes from his as she continued. She couldn't take the intimacy in his eyes, the questions, or the reassurance. She had things to say that couldn't wait any longer.

"The three of us were sitting downstairs at the dining table, joking around, when suddenly I caught your eyes. I saw love and helplessness mixed together and I could feel my heart melt. The thought of you hurt, the thought of Kale hurt, in anyway almost killed a part of me. I ran and have hated myself every day for it. I will not do that again. I will not live regretting anything. Most of all the way I feel for you."

She didn't know what brought on the outpour, other than the fact that she didn't want to keep anything from him. Especially what she felt inside, what told her this was their time, no matter what Jerry did. They either died in each other's arms or loved each other for the rest of their lives.

"Look at me Sonja." She could hear a little of the father tone in his voice. She opened her eyes to find him perfectly serious, no humor, no empathy, just honesty, and the love she had seen before.

"I loved you then and I love you now. No matter what anyone says, they can't stop that. No matter what anyone does, they can't stop that. Jerry could torture me to death and my last thought would be how much I love you—and to come back from the grave to kill him." He was happy to see her laugh at that.

"I'm sorry that it took so long for me to straighten myself out and see that... Nothing on this earth means more to me than you."

"I love you. And since we are being completely open, every time I've ever called you darlin', I was really wanting to say 'I love you.'"

"I always wondered why you called me darling so much."

He smiled, but didn't correct the way she said it.

"Darlin' I like it," she said. "Now we need to decide if we are getting out of this bed or if we are . . . staying in this bed."

"A year huh . . .?"

"Yes. And you have been driving me insane for more than the past few weeks that I've lived here."

"I don't sympathize with that. I've been chasing you for three years."

"Chasing?" She tried to sound astonished. "Not very hard."

"You were with Jerry. I had to respect your wishes, your life. My brother wagging after you too didn't help that matter."

"Wagging? That's a funny way to put it. He really does like Layla and Jerry hurt her."

He watched as the smile faded, replaced by pain.

"It wasn't your fault, darlin'. We all now know he is insane."

"I never thought about him going after anyone but me. Well, you and Kale. But I figured you two could take care of yourselves if you knew it was coming."

"We can and will. He will never get to you again."

"I know. I know because you say it."

He kissed her. He couldn't stop kissing her. Nothing on this earth would ever stop him from kissing her again.

"While it's light outside you should get some sleep." Her mind was moving and moving quickly.

"I want to keep kissing you."

"You need the rest and we don't need you comatose."

He rolled away from her, she slid out of his bed, and got dressed, forgetting the underwear somewhere in his bed.

"I'll go clean something."

"Wake me for anything."

She looked at him laying in bed staring at her. She wanted to not let him sleep, but he needed it. She shut and locked the windows and left the room.

Sonja kept busy, mostly cleaning anything and everything to keep moving. More than once she was tempted to go back upstairs and have fun waking him up. The closest she got was the bedroom door. Twenty minutes she stood there watching him sleep, hoping he was having a good dream.

It was almost ten when she starting making a light dinner. She chose sandwiches since there would be little to no noise to distract her from sounds of the house. She didn't hum or talk to herself. She listened to everything. Part of her was thankful for every second of silence that went by. Part of her prayed to get it over with. With everything set out on the kitchen island, she made the sandwiches, slowly. He needed every minute of sleep she could let him have.

The noise didn't make her jump but it did send her heart racing. It came from above her head, from Nick's room. She wiped her hands on the towel, discarding it for the sword on the dining room table. The noise came again as she dashed up the stairs two at a time, she glanced to the bottom of the T as she passed. Holding the sword at her waist in both hands she went in the bedroom.

Nick pushed the sword to the side and leaned back a little still wiping the sleep from his eyes. "Nice to see you too darlin'."

"You made noise, a lot of it. Sounded like more than just you up here."

"You were with me until I woke up."

"You are sweet."

"And loveable." He pulled her to him, kissing her.

"Dinner downstairs, sandwiches."

"Me, you, bed."

"Food before your metabolism eats you alive."

"I'd rather eat you alive."

She couldn't help but think the bed would be a good idea as he kissed down her neck. Then his stomach growled and they laughed. His stomach got the last word. She went downstairs to finish fixing the makeshift dinner, he joined her a few minutes later.

They stood in the kitchen, smiling and chatting using the island between them as a table and barrier. She loved looking at him, his eyes wild with thoughts of taking her back upstairs. The short five hours of sleep did him well but she was paying the price for not joining him.

They finished eating and she started to clean. "I think you have had enough mindless cleaning for one day."

He grabbed her hand, pulling her into his arms. She felt weightless between no sleep and the affects he had on her body, having problems keeping her eyes open and her brain functioning.

His kisses didn't stop as he pulled her out of the kitchen, through the dining room. At the stairs, he had to stop kissing her, taking both her hands in his, he led her up the stairs. This time he didn't scan the windows for signs of someone, he kept his eyes on hers.

They moved in silence through the house as though they could read each other's mind. A few feet from his room, he broke the silence as he stopped for a moment.

"Close your eyes."

She did as he asked, "Not sure that's safe I might fall asleep."

"I will keep you awake." She followed his voice and where his hands led her. Her breath caught as he began removing her shirt. "Keep them closed for another moment."

Her body shook as she stood naked, unable to see what he was doing. She heard soft music begin before he touched her again. He lifted her up, laying her gently on the bed, kissing whatever was closest to his lips as they moved across her skin. She felt him move onto the bed.

"Open."

Her eyes opened to reveal soft candlelight filling the room. The candlesticks he bought her on top of the headboard, others on his dresser, along the open windowsill, even scattered about on the floor. Soft music drifting from the radio. Nick watching her face, as he sat on the end of the bed, waiting, desperately hoping for her approval.

They sat there for what felt like an eternity until he watched her blink too slow, as one tear fell from her eye.

"Oh, Sonja don't cry." He crawled across the bed, taking her in his arm, kissing her cheek, while her body shook.

"This is the most beautiful . . . romantic . . ."

"Thank you, darlin'."

"I love you, Nick."

"I want you, Sonja. No, matter what I tell myself about timing. I want you."

"I am yours."

He pulled back, meeting her smiling eyes.

Nick kissed her as he pulled the covers over them. Their hands explored their bodies, each making mental lists of the reactions of a touch here or there. They lost themselves in each other, anyone outside of that room no longer existed, only the two of them alone on the planet. Sweet words whispering from their lips when they were freed.

He wrapped his arms around her, kissing her neck, marveling at how breathless she was. Revealing in the feel of her against him, he knew he couldn't hold himself together anymore. "Sonja, darlin', tell me . . ."

"No where else I belong."

"No one else, but you."

She wrapped her body around him as he gently pushed, a deep breath and muted sound from her stopped him as he continued to kiss her neck. His heart broke thinking he hurt her.

His eyes scanned her face as her lips gently moved with no sound escaping. "Sonja?"

She opened her eyes, moving to gently take his lips, still trying to find the words. "Darling, don't stop."

His heart started beating again, cautiously. He continued to skim her lips as he did just as she asked. Each time he moved, ever so slightly her breath would shudder, causing his muscles to twitch, causing her to shudder again. She couldn't help but giggle, as their bodies spoke the odd language.

"Giggling is not helping me, my love." He pushed again, watching as she tried to breathe, the giggle replaced by a look of pleasure across her face, muscles going taunt in her body. "Sonja?"

"Again."

Hollywood had nothing on them.

They moved silently, together. Careful of each other's reactions, adapting, enjoying.

He stared as she slowly drifted away, words of love, whispering in her ear between kisses. She so thrilled him, satisfied him that sleep was the farthest thing from his mind and body. His arms wrapped around her, he watched as the few remaining candles burned themselves out, as the clock ticked three.

Sonja woke to Nick's lips massaging the back of her neck. She opened her eyes to find her hiding under her own hair. A moan of pleasure poured out of her.

"Good morning, darlin'."

"Nick." His name sang from her lips as he gently rolled her to her back. The clock claimed it was seven in the morning as he kissed across her chest.

"Seven?" She tried to sit up astonished at the time

"Forget it." He said pushing her back to the bed with the weight of his body.

"But you should have been gone already." Flowed from her lips as her breathing became erratic.

"Not today."

"Nick?"

"I tried, I couldn't. Too much to think about. I want you."

She could feel the urgency again in his lips, feel his muscles taunt with holding himself back from taking her. So caught up in his body she could hardly get out one word, "Plan?"

"Not today. Not now. Need more." It was probably the first time in his life, that his brain didn't have some kind of plan or working on one.

"Insatiable!"

"For you, yes." He took her, in pure passion, he didn't ask, only responded to her body.

It was almost ten when he crawled out of bed to the shower. Nick let the cold water wash over him, as he sat on the floor, trying to find where his mind had gone. All the planning went straight out of his head when he saw her lying in his bed this morning, naked, and knowing he could take her. Three years of passion had poured out of him, through him, and into Sonja. Three years of sexual frustration quenched, and he loved every second of it. By the smile on her face, he judged she felt the same. If he ever found where his brain went he would remember to ask, to make sure she enjoyed it as much as he had. To make sure he hadn't hurt her.

Sonja wanted to grab him as he crawled away, but her body was having a problem moving. Somehow, she found the strength to roll over. Her mind wandered aimlessly as she watched the squirrels chase each other through the branches of the old oak. She couldn't help it as the grin came across her face, everything was right with the world, even if that world consisted only of the room she was in and the squirrels in the oak.

Then she saw him through the floor length windows, standing in the yard staring straight at her, watching her. She didn't scream, she didn't even flinch, she glared back.

Now she understood love, friendship, and true fear. She didn't fear Jerry. She only feared living without Nick. The thought of waking one day without him next to her for the rest of her life hurt. Jerry fueled her anger.

She jumped out of bed, not caring she was naked, not worried that her muscles hurt. She grabbed the bow, unlocked, and flung open the window. She took aim as he dashed across the backyard, sending the arrow flying as he ducked into the trees. He escaped her deadly accurate arrow by a bare fraction of a second.

She began to scream out of the window. "Go to hell, leave us alone. You sick . . ."

She quit screaming and started crying as Nick wrapped her in his towel and arms.

"He's watching . . . He was really watching us." She stammered as the tears leveled out.

"It's almost over, darlin'."

"Tomorrow you leave on time?"

"Yes. Today though, you are mine. No matter what he does."

"One day or the rest of our lives."

"That's the thought."

"Food then more."

16.

Sonja crawled out of the hot bath, wrapped her hair in a towel, and slipped on her pajamas. There was no reason to get dressed since she was just going downstairs to the chair and wait.

Nick left almost twenty minutes before and she should have gotten out of the bath then but her muscles hurt, it was a good hurt. Never in her life had she felt so good and no one was going to rob her of that feeling.

She spent some of the time in the tub mentally preparing for a fight. The last forty-eight hours of her life fueling her, her anger fueling her. She opened the door to the bathroom, still drying her hair, crossed the hall into her room, and put on a pair of socks. She bounced down the stairs deciding she would grab a quick bite to eat before taking her chair. When her feet touched the landing, she saw him out the corner of her eye. At first she was ready to yell at Nick for coming back. Then she saw him fully, his wild eyes staring at her from the kitchen doorway.

"Fresh from a hot bath, Sonja?"

"Go to hell."

"Oh you are in no position to talk like that." He laughed almost hysterically, remembering Nick taunting him with those very words.

She glimpsed the butcher knife in his hand as he came out of the archway. She took her chance, sliding across the hardwood floor on her side of the dining room table, grabbing the sword next to the couch.

She turned, placing the sword across his neck as he leaned backwards. "He will protect me."

"He isn't going to get the chance." They stared each other down, each smiling at their own little secret. "What? You think I've been watching and didn't know he's sitting in the back pasture, in a tree, with binoculars, waiting for me to come near you?"

Sonja's smile faded. "What did you do?"

"Nothing yet, wait for it and you will find out."

She looked out the back door, standing wide open. It was the best place to see the chair that she spent one day sitting in and was supposed to sit in today. She was standing in between the door and the chair. Jerry had been standing in that path before she came down. Nick knew he was there.

"Nick . . ." She started to yell 'don't," her words were cut short as the knife crossed her side. She pushed the sword, sinking it into his shoulder instead of his neck.

"Stupid bitch." Jerry screamed through a tight jaw.

"Nick don't." She managed to get it all out, as she felt the side of her body dampen. She assumed it was her blood but she wasn't going to look and find out. She didn't need to pass out and make things worse.

Jerry lunged at her with the knife. This time she caught his other shoulder, amazed at how easily the sword slid into his body. He screamed again.

She heard the gunshot echo through the house from the backyard. Her body wanted to pass out as her brain played the scene in the back of the house: Nick running through the field, trying to get to her; a gunman setup by Jerry, lying in wait; Nick's body falling limp to the ground. She felt the tears fall.

"That's right Sonja, he's gone. That little

brother of his is next. Well, after I take you away. Do everything I've ever wanted to."

Anger burst forth in her—everything Jerry had ever said or done fueling her. Everything Nick meant to her fueled her. She lunged at him this time, slicing into his left side. She pulled the sword back, watching as the blood gushed from of the newest wound. Her mind was clear, moving, she was nowhere near passing out.

"It's over Sonja," he yelled, futilely pressing his hand against the gash. "You have nothing to fight for anymore." He ran the knife down the blade of her sword she smacked it way.

"If one hair on his head is harmed, you will die anyway. Might as well be from me."

She was trying her hardest not to believe the images in her head. Not to believe the words from Jerry. The sound of Nick's heart was her new fuel, the strong, steady beat, in the casing to match.

Nick watched and waited. The old deer stand made a good perch for his own spying. This morning he didn't have to wait long. Jerry brazenly walked across the backyard and up the stairs, staring straight at Nick as he went. The bastard knew he was sitting there. He knew he was waiting for him and still went straight for the house instead of taking him out first.

Nick jumped out of the tree as Jerry took a hammer to the back door. Nick was careful to keep his head in the tall grass. The tan colored wheat hiding him well, his hair under one of Kale's work hats so it would not give away his position.

Nick found the guy waiting on the side of the horse trailer for him to come running through the backyard. He raised his bow, waited and counted, and let go. He watched as the arrow struck the man in the arm. He missed his intended target by the slightest margin. The man's neck still intact. The would-be attacker yanked the arrow from of his arm, let out a yelp and began looking around, the gun held high.

Nick crawled across the ground knowing he had to hurry. Sonja was in more danger than he was. He wasn't even sure which part of the house she was in when Jerry went in the back door. He slowed when the grass thinned out enough for him to see again. He took another shot, nailing the gunmen in the leg.

The man sent a bullet flying in return. It was a lucky shot that skimmed Nick's ear. He heard it go by as his heart stopped beating for a second. It was close, too close. He crawled to where he could come out on the other side of the trailer with tall grass the entire way. He kept his head low watching the man's feet come to the end of the trailer. He hoped the element of surprise would be enough. Easing to his side of the trailer he jumped out.

Sonja tried to take a deep breath but her side was beginning to weigh her down. Her brain still moving, she needed to get to Nick if he was wounded. Another shot from the backyard brought a wicked smile to her face. "Told you he's not dead."

Jerry stabbed at her again. She was ready. She lunged at him with the sword, felt it sink, then sink farther still. He screamed, a scream of pure pain as he fell back. Sonja threw all her weight against the sword. She pulled it back and did it again. Tears streamed from her eyes as she forced it home again. Falling to the floor, she crawled toward the kitchen away from the dying body thrashing on the floor behind her. The thought that she might not make it to the back door crossed her mind as she held her side, feeling blood oozing from her wound. Only whispers coming out of her mouth. Only one word.

"Nick."

Nick used his bow to hit the gunmen straight in the face, then shattered the fiberglass as he knocked the gun from his hand. He hit the guy twice straight in the middle of his nose before the man fell down. Possessed, Nick stomped the man's face with his boots until he quit moving. Then kicked him in the ribs for good measure, to make sure he wasn't faking. The blood streaming from his nose, forehead, and mouth told Nick the guy was out. He took the gun and ran for the back door. Yelling for Sonja.

He came in the door to find her on the floor, blood dribbling from her side, tears streaming down her face. Her eyes were open and staring at him, relief flashing.

He grabbed a stack of towels, putting them under her hand, over the wound then picked her up. "It's okay, darlin' I'm here. Please stop crying. That can't be good for blood loss."

"I heard the gun. I thought you were dead."

"Can't get rid of me that easy, darlin'"

He laid her on her good side on the picnic table. Kissed her lips, "I am going to get the car, you stay right here."

"I will." She didn't have the energy to tell him she couldn't go anywhere. The less he knew about how she was doing at this point the better.

He took off running through the field. Pulling out his cell phone, he called Detective Ivan.

On the other, someone answered and spoke: "We are already on our way!"

Nick closed the phone before he neared the car. He jumped in and started it. He put it in drive and pushed the little car through the scrubs, fence, and small trees. He didn't let up on the gas pedal until he was in the backyard. He yanked the emergency brake, jumped out the car, and picked her up. He sat her carefully in the back seat thankful for the convertible. "Talk to me Sonja."

"Nick."

"That will do, just keep saying it. Makes me think of last night. Just keep saying it."

He listened to her say it as he peeled out of the driveway. He wasn't going to pull over for anything other than an ambulance and he was moving fast. The T-junction came quickly, but he didn't touch the brake, just shifted through the gears. He spun the tires and the car slid sideways as he passed the front of the detective's car, shifting back into the higher gear.

Detective Ivan had his sirens going from the moment he heard dispatch on his radio: "Shots fired near the Badeaux house."

The sight of Sonja's car gave him hope—until he saw Nick driving, a man possessed and Sonja unconscious in the back seat.

When he arrived at the house, he verified the man outside was alive and unconscious. Jerry, on the floor of the dining room, had not been so lucky. The huge pool of blood he was lying in told the detective before he got close enough to double-check the pulse. The second pool in the kitchen was the one that worried him. Along with the drips that led to it, he estimated almost two pints on that trail. He grabbed his radio as an officer identified Sonja's car driving erratically and not responding to lights or siren. The detective yelled above everyone else on the radio, identified himself, and told the officer to escort that car to the hospital. The channel grew quiet.

The detective barked out orders to the arriving officers. He was headed toward his car when he saw a familiar SUV pull into the driveway. He updated Kale as much as he could, as much as he knew, before Kale put the truck in reverse and took off. The detective didn't catch up until he was in the parking lot of the hospital.

Nick didn't care if the officer was in front of or behind him. Nothing was going to stop him. Hearing her whisper his name pushed him to go faster. He pulled the emergency brake again as he arrived in front of the hospital. He didn't care that he was blocking half the driveway, nor that it was still running. If someone took her car he would buy her another. He jumped out on the passenger's side and gently pulled her into his arms, the pool of blood on the seat drew tears to his eyes. The towels she had been holding fell away. Only his name from her lips still gave him hope. His name was softer, slower but it was still coming from her.

He burst through the doors yelling for help. Three nurses and a doctor were already there. He half made a mental note to thank the detective for that. He explained it was a knife wound as he laid her on the stretcher. As they wheeled her down the hall, he heard her whisper his name one final time. One of the nurses grabbed him and he almost took a swing at her. He ran his hand through his hair as his tears began to fall.

In that instant it came to him that he couldn't remember ever crying in his life. He slid down the wall and began to sob.

Running through the parking lot, Kale wondered if anything would have been different if he hadn't dropped off Layla before coming home. He watched an officer get out of Sonja's car. The detective was heading to the car instead of the emergency room.

He started for the nurses' station until he saw Nick pacing the hall, covered in blood.

"Nick!" It didn't sound like his own voice echoing down the hall, the panic overwhelming the sound. He stood in front of his brother, who couldn't talk instead wrapping his arms around Kale. Kale could feel his brother's chest heaving.

Kale walked Nick to the waiting room, sitting him in a chair before asking the detective to help keep them updated on her condition. Kale stood back and watched Nick for a moment. Never in his life had he seen his brother unable to talk. Unable to control his emotions. Never distraught over anything. If there had ever been any doubt in his mind that Nick loved her or she him, it was gone. Kale took his seat next to his brother, wrapping his arm around Nick's shoulder trying his best to give some support, even while his own heart was breaking.

Nick recognized the nurse as she came down the hall with the detective. He stood, knowing he looked worse than the last time he had met her.

"Nurse Wilkins."

"Hello." She didn't know what to say but she knew she couldn't take long. The man looked like he had gone to hell and back. He wasn't the scary man standing at the end of a bed, he was little more than a child.

"She lost a lot of blood."

Nick's legs weakened and he sat back down, his

heartbeat disappearing.

"Almost four pints. She's asleep. Other than that, we don't know how it's gonna turn out."

"She's alive though?"

He had prepared for the worst, hoped for the best. The realization that she was alive hadn't fully registered yet.

"Yes. As long as the two of you are quiet, you can come in and see her. But understand she needs sleep."

Nick stood, quickly wrapping his arms around the short women. "Thank you."

"While you sit in there, why don't we look at those knuckles and your ear. What kind of fight was this anyway?"

"One for love."

17.

Sonja woke with a dull pain in her side that instantly grew sharp if she moved in the least. She didn't have to open her eyes to figure out she was in the hospital. The last thing she remembered was being wheeled away, while a nurse kept Nick out of the emergency room, him covered in her blood. She opened her eyes to find Kale sitting on the side of her bed, smiling that she was awake.

"About time. We've been worried about you."

She tried to talk, finding her throat too dry to get any sound out. Kale dropped a few ice chips in her mouth. "Sorry it's the best we can do right now. Strict orders. No beer."

"Where . . ." Her voice breathy, harsh.

"He couldn't sit here staring at you not moving anymore."

"Bad?"

"Nick is fine. His knuckles are a little bruised, but nothing that won't fix itself in a few days. You're gonna live and have a nice scar across your rib cage for it."

"Jerry?"

"Dead." Kale watched as Sonja's eyes closed. "Detective is keeping you both out of jail. At least as long as you don't try to leave the state."

They sat in silence while she contemplated the last few weeks of her life.

"Okay, I can't see anything, but I'm back."

Nick's voice opened her eyes instantly. He was walking into the room blind folded, in his brother's clothes. She smiled as she put her finger to her lips.

"What are you doing Nick?" Kale had the father tone now.

"I can't stand to see her like this, so I won't look." Kale moved to the doorway to help direct his brother to sit on her good side, close to her. "Anything change?"

"Not much."

"I think she's been asleep long enough."

"You kept her awake for the better part of three days. I think she needed it." Kale slowly pushed his brother closer to her. "Not to mention, you let her lose four pints of blood..."

"Shut up. It was her plan and could have gone worse. You want to put her hand in mine so I can tell when there is a change in her?"

Kale reached over, helping her to sit up a little further until her lips touched Nick's.

Nick jumped off the bed, pulling the blindfold as Kale gently helped her lay back on the bed.

"Good to see you my darling."

"Darlin'." He wrapped his arms around her kissing her cheek.

"I love you too." He felt her body jump a little with pain.

"I'm sorry, I can't even touch you without hurting you."

"Sure you can, just not my left side."

He touched her lips with his, keeping his hands on the bed. "Here?"

"Good."

He moved to her cheek, then her neck. "Here?"

"Hmm... Good."

"I think I will just go find a nurse or something." Kale said as he turned for the door.

"Kale!" They said together.

"Sorry. That is going to take a little bit to get used to."

Sonja motioned him to come nearer to her. He moved to the left side of her bed and stared down at her. She motioned again as if she wanted to whisper in his ear. He put his head down to hers. She kissed his cheek and said, "Thank you."

"You are welcome. Now keep those lips to yourself. No kissing on my brother then me. It's wrong somehow. Like I'm kissing on my brother or something."

Sonja laughed then grabbed her side and grimaced. "You're trying to kill me."

A nurse came in the room, "Good evening, sleepy head."

Sonja met her smile with one of her own. "When can I go home?"

"Listen to this little girl. Just woke up after sleepin' for almost sixteen hours and wants to go home."

"Sixteen hours?" She looked at Nick, apologetic for what he must have gone through in that amount of time.

"Yes, a severe knife wound will do that to a person. You have to stay for a few days for observations, then a doctor will decide when you're ready."

"This is Nurse Wilkins, Sonja. She likes your handiwork." Kale said with a good laugh as his brother smiled.

"My handiwork?"

"Oh yes, child. I would have killed the bastard

the first time."

"She was the nurse on duty when we visited another patient." It only took a second and Sonja caught up.

"I think you better keep this one, sweetie. Not very many people scare me. He did the first time I met him. Then the second time he hugged me and tried his best not to cry, just so you know. Now I think I kinda like him, too."

Sonja laughed with a tear in her eye. It hurt to think that Nick might have actually cried for her. She grabbed her side again.

"Did I mention no laughing. It kinda hurts."

"Doctor will be in shortly."

Nurse Wilkins left the room with a laugh as Kale said, "Thank you ma'am."

"Kale, leave the room a minute." Sonja was perfectly serious.

"Actually I'm going home." He walked over, pushed his brother out of the way, kissed her forehead, then hugged Nick. Adding as he went out the door. "Be good or the nurse will make him leave."

"You want me all to yourself darlin'?" Nick leaned down to her, running his hands through her hair.

"Every day for the rest of my life. I'm sorry again that I put you through all this."

"Don't be. There is no place I belong other than with you. Even with all the trouble you are."

"I promise to never make you cry—or come close to it—again."

"I'm not sure that is a promise you can keep. I can think of a few things that could make me cry in this life." He watched as her eyes started to droop, knowing the nurse slipped her a little painkiller in her IV. "Sleep well, darlin'."

Sonja spent three days in the hospital before the doctor allowed her to go home. Nick didn't leave the room again. He pushed the extra bed right next to hers and kept a hold of her hand whether she was awake or asleep.

Before Sonja came home, Kale took the rug out of the dining room and disposed of it. He replaced it with one that Layla suggested. He even scrubbed all the blood off the floor. Not to bad for his first cleaning experience. He did a good job, considering how disgusting it was. He and Layla picked up Nick's car and dropped off Sonja's for a new paint job, a little body work, and hopefully to get all the blood out of it. They moved half her bedroom to his, leaving the rest for storage in what was now the extra room. Kale thought he might offer it to Layla.

Nurse Wilkins came in a few minutes early to see Sonja off. She wheeled her to the door while Nick got the car. They each gave the nurse a hug, then he picked Sonja up and sat her in the Mustang. He gently reached across and buckled her in, kissing her before he sat back in his own seat. "You ready to go home, darlin'?"

"With you, anytime." She sang on the way home as she watched him drive.

He carried her into the house and straight to his room. Waited on her hand and foot for the next week, pushing her back in the bed when she objected, until he felt she was healed enough to move on her own. Then they each went back to work. Jack threw her a party and she actually socialized with everyone. She started on two new accounts that week. Life overall returned to normal. She slept in Nick's arms every night, waking with a kiss every morning. They were just waiting to go to court and trying to stay out of jail.

Detective Ivan tried to explain everything to them about self-defense and defense of your home. The problem was, she killed Jerry with a sword and Nick broke almost every bone in the other guys face. There were a lot of people who found the brutality extreme. Everyone just had to wait for the court day four weeks away.

They didn't think about it, didn't dwell, they lived each day like the next didn't exist.

"Ms. Sonja Mitchell."

The bailiff's voice rang through the small courtroom as she stood, letting Nick's hand slip out of hers only when she was too far away. Her heart pounded as she stepped through the swinging divider, glancing at the man behind the lawyers' desk as confidently as she could. She stood in front of the judge waiting patiently, fighting the darkness that wanted to engulf her.

"Are you a God fearing woman, Ms. . . . Mitchell?"

"I believe I am. Yes sir."

"Bailiff."

"Do you swear to tell the truth and whole truth, to the best of your ability?" The bailiff's voice echoed again in the quiet room.

"Yes sir." She said, a little intimidated.

"Why is a person looking at murder charges not in handcuffs?"

"Self-defense." Her lawyer quickly piped in.

"Let the girl answer for herself."

She smiled at the judge. This was her kind of man, didn't take lip from anyone. Even if the lawyer was on her side.

Her smile faded quickly as the judge looked her up and down. Then back to the file. "Engagement ring on that finger?"

"Yes, Your Honor." The smile was back, the ring had only been there a few hours, but she was sure she was glowing.

"You have that much faith in your innocence?"

"I have that much faith in fate and the justice system, sir."

"The man couldn't wait until today was over?"

"Life is short, sir."

"Says here you ran a man through with a sword? A couple times?" The judge's voice sounded confused, his wrinkled brow added to it.

"Yes sir, I did."

The judge quickly looked up from the file to meet her eyes as her lawyer threw down the file. "How?"

"Pointy end first and push."

"That sounds like a smart remark, young lady."

"It was not meant to be, Your Honor. Before my friend handed me a sword, that is how he told me to defend myself if I ever had to."

"Would that friend be Mr. Nicolas Badeaux?"

"Yes, Your Honor, it would be."

"Isn't he next on my docket for excessive force?"

"Not sure about next Your Honor, but 'yes' on the charge."

"I was not speaking to you Ms. Mitchell."

"Yes sir."

The clerk spoke quickly. "Yes, Judge, he is."

"Is Mr. Badeaux in the courtroom?"

"Yes sir, a few of them," she replied. "Oh, I'm sorry. You weren't speaking to me were you?"

"No, I was not. Nicolas Badeaux might as well come up here so we only go through this once."

Nick quickly and quietly joined Sonja in front of the judge, grabbing her left hand as soon as he was near enough. He felt her ring, knowing he couldn't have been wrong. Fate, destiny, and God wouldn't let them be together, let them survive, only to rip them apart again.

"Mr. Badeaux, are you a God-fearing man?"

"More so every day, sir." He didn't add since the day she knocked on his front door.

"Bailiff."

"Do you swear to tell the truth and whole truth, to the best of your ability?"

"Yes sir." Nick said.

"Good, who wants to explain this all to me?"

Nick and Sonja looked at each other, smiled.

"I dated Jerry for three years. He hit me one too many times..."

"She came to stay with my brother and me ..."

"Jerry had someone put a brick through his car window..."

"He tried to have her kidnapped..."

"Shot his brother..."

"Attempted to shoot me..."

"All because I kissed him..." She motioned to Nick.

"Attacked her best friend..."

"We made her and his brother leave town..."

"We fell in love..."

"Jerry tried to kill me..."

"Big guy tried to shoot me when I tried to save her..."

"I killed Jerry with a sword..."

"I beat the big guy until he quit moving..."

"He took me to the hospital for wounds Jerry caused…"

"Now we are standing in front of you…"

"Anything we can explain further, Your Honor?" They spoke in unison.

The judge sat back, looking at young couple. Their hands clamped together so tight their knuckles turning white. Nick's fingers gently playing with the diamond on the ring.

"A sword?"

"Renaissance fighting, Your Honor…" Sonja quickly jumped in.

"Me and my brother practice in the backyard. You are welcome to come watch anytime…"

"They beat on each other until someone gives…"

"She's a good student…"

"No, he's a good teacher…"

"Stop!" The judge ordered.

"Sorry, Your Honor." They said in unison.

"At least that was less like a tennis match. I am guessing that is your ring on her finger?"

"Yes sir. Like she said, life is short…"

"Why put off the inevitable…" Sonja added.

"Stop!" The judge read the files over one more time, while they stood silent watching him. "How many witnesses to these events?"

"Each incident has a police report, sir." Nick didn't interrupt her as she continued, "There were at least five officers that responded to the original police call. Five, plus the detective for the broken window. Two plus the detective for the guy who tried to kidnap me. Almost twenty for him shooting Kale because it was very public. Plus the forty to one hundred bystanders on that. Then another ten officers for the finale. Some of those officers could have been repeats. Then add emergency room doctors and staff of the hospital for each visit."

The judge could see she was counting off in her head to make sure she didn't miss any. "Seems about right so forty to two hundred all in all, plus me, him, his brother and Layla."

"That's impressive. Is Detective Ivan in the courtroom?"

"Here, Your Honor." The detective stood up but didn't approach.

"Layla McKenzie?"

"Yes sir."

"Kaleb Badeaux?"

"Yes sir." Each person stood as they were called.

"Any additional people who witnessed some part of what these two have explained?" Sonja and Nick half turned around to watch most of the room stand.

"Anyone want to add anything to their story?"

The room stayed quiet, causing the judge to look up from the files again, "All these people and no one has anything to add?"

The room remained quiet.

"Sit!" Everyone did as instructed.

"Anyone want to act as character witnesses for these two?" The judge looked up as every person in the room stood including her lawyer.

"Counsel?"

"Ms. Mitchell is my sister-in-law, Your Honor."

"I see. Sit please." The judge stared the two down, for what felt like an eternity.

"Does the State have anything to add?"

"They each admit to their crime, Your Honor. The states' position is excessive force on both parts.

Self defense, but still excessive."

Sonja's brother-in-law jumped up, happy he could finally do his job. "Your Honor, Mr. Lane cut her with a knife, resulting in the loss of four pints of blood in a very short period of time. Mr. Badeaux simply stopped his victim from shooting him."

"Thank you, Counsel, I read the files." The judge sat back looking over the room. He could send it to trial and off his shoulders.

"It is in the opinion of this court that since neither defendant has a record, since every bit of evidence indicates self defense, that both Ms. Sonja Mitchell and Mr. Nicolas Badeaux are exonerated of all charges."

No one in the room moved, except the prosecuting attorney, who picked up his briefcase and coat.

"Sonja. Nick." The couple turned to her brother-in-law, "That means you can celebrate."

"Completely?" Nick wanted to clarify. They looked at each other in shock.

"Counsel you don't want to object?" The judge spoke over everyone, as the other lawyer was almost to the door

"No, Your Honor. I do not."

The judge looked back to Nick, "Yes completely son, and I hope to never see a case like this again."

"Thank you, Your Honor." They said in unison.

"One more question before you leave. How do you do that? My wife and I have been married for forty years and can't even hold a conversation."

"We just know." They laughed a little this time, understanding that nothing could ever pull them apart again.

Made in the USA